STRANGER AT
ST BRIDE'S

Staffroom at St Bride's Series #2

Debbie Young

Copyright Information

Stranger at St Bride's – A Staffroom at St Bride's
Mystery by Debbie Young
© Debbie Young 2020
Published by Hawkesbury Press 2020
Hawkesbury Upton, Gloucestershire, England

Cover design by Rachel Lawston of Lawston Design

ISBN (paperback) 978-1-911223-59-7

Also available as an ebook

About the Author

Debbie Young writes warm, witty, feel-good fiction.

Her Staffroom at St Bride's Mystery series will follow an extraordinary English girls' boarding school for an academic year. Her Sophie Sayers Village Mystery series of seven novels runs the course of a village year from one summer to the next in the fictional Cotswold village of Wendlebury Barrow.

Her humorous short stories are available in themed collections, such as *Marry in Haste*, *Quick Change* and *Stocking Fillers*, or as single story mini-books, such as *The Natter of Knitters* and *Lighting Up Time*, and in many anthologies.

She is a frequent speaker at literature festivals and writing events and is founder and director of the free Hawkesbury Upton Literature Festival.

A regular contributor to two local community magazines, the award-winning *Tetbury Advertiser* and the *Hawkesbury Parish News*, she has published two collections of her columns, *Young by Name* and *All Part of the Charm*. These publications offer insight into her own life in a small Cotswold village where she lives with her Scottish husband and their teenage daughter.

For the latest information about Debbie's
books and events, visit her Writing Life website,
where you may also like to join her free Readers' Club.
www.authordebbieyoung.com

STRANGER AT ST BRIDE'S

A Staffroom at St Bride's Story

1

Gemma Meets a Ghost

"Miss Lamb, Miss Lamb, there's a ghost outside the front door!"

At St Bride's School for Girls, I never quite know what to expect when I open the staffroom door to deal with a girl's enquiry, but Imogen's announcement before the first lesson of the day was unprecedented.

"Foolish child," muttered Mavis Brook, the geography teacher, from behind me, closing the exercise book she was marking. "I blame that Halloween nonsense for putting such silly ideas into her head. Most unhealthy."

The terror on Imogen's face made me loath to dismiss her claim as a prank, although that seemed more likely than seeing a real ghost. I tried to make light of the situation to calm her down.

"Anyone's ghost in particular? Are you sure it's not just one of your friends in a white sheet?"

Imogen shook her head vigorously.

"Oh no, miss, it's a real ghost all right. You should see it. It's far too tall to be any of my friends. And it's a man."

Imogen, aged 11, came up only as far as my shoulder, but there were some very tall girls in the top class of seventeen- to eighteen-year-olds. Might one of those try such a stunt?

"OK, Imogen, wait a moment and I'll take a look out of the staffroom window to see whether it's still there."

I closed the door – school policy is to keep the staffroom private from the girls – and crossed to the big bay window that gave on to the forecourt. As I peered round to view the front porch, the doorbell rang again, and a tall, thin, dark-haired man with a wide clipped moustache stepped back to look around for signs of life.

Nearby on the window seat, Oriana Bliss, Head of Maths, looked up from a stationery catalogue she had been browsing through and followed my gaze.

"He looks like flesh and blood to me."

"Well, you're the expert," said PE teacher Joe Spryke, unzipping his pink tracksuit top. Joe is a former competitive cyclist on the run from hostile journalists who unfairly blamed him for an international sports scandal. During term-time, Joe disguises himself as a woman to escape detection.

I narrowed my eyes to focus better on the stranger. I had to agree with Oriana.

"He looks familiar, but I don't think he's one of the girls' fathers, is he?"

Oriana laid her catalogue down on the seat beside her.

"Not unless the Bursar's signed up a new pupil during the half-term holiday. And speaking of the Bursar, where is he? Why isn't he answering that pesky doorbell?"

In the absence of a budget that would stretch to a receptionist, answering the door falls to the Bursar, the only official man in the school besides Max Security (not his real name, of course – like Joe, he's incognito). Max is like St Bride's own Scarlet Pimpernel. You never knew where he might pop up next, and it is often in the place you least expect. The Bursar is far more visible, an overt equivalent to Max's undercover agent – a kind of bouncer, perhaps. The Bouncing Bursar. I smiled. Perhaps he wasn't so bad after all, now I'd got used to him.

The bell rang for the third time. Oriana glanced at the wall clock above the door, then at me. There were just a few minutes left before lessons began for the day. I took her hint.

"I suppose I can let him in myself."

Imogen, still waiting outside the staffroom door, skipped alongside me as I strode down the corridor to the entrance hall.

"Oh miss, you are brave! Do you want me to get a gang of girls to rescue you in case it's the dangerous kind of ghost?"

I tried not to hurt her dignity by laughing. She meant well.

"I'm sure I'll be fine, thank you. I don't think much harm can come to me answering the front door in broad daylight."

"Ooh, yes, thank goodness it's daylight. That means he can't be a vampire. But I'll hide nearby, just in case. If you

3

need me, shout the code word. What should our code word be?"

After spending half-term with my parents, I hadn't yet retuned to the girls' mindset.

"How about 'help'?"

Imogen frowned.

"I don't think you're really trying, miss."

When we reached the vast entrance hall that had so intimidated me on my arrival at the school back in September, Imogen took cover behind one of the broad marble pillars supporting the ornate painted ceiling. I marched across the tiled floor, heels clicking, and heaved open the front door.

"Good morning," I said, blinking against the pale November sunshine. "How can I help you, sir?"

The stranger stepped forward, assuming I'd let him in. We did an awkward shuffle as I tried to stall him until I'd established his credentials. We're very hot on child protection at St Bride's, even with members of school staff. Max Security lives in Rose Lodge, one of the pair of cottages at the entrance to the main drive, and has security cameras all over the place. In the other cottage, Honeysuckle Lodge, lives the Bursar. Thus, even the two men at the heart of school life are in their leisure time kept at a distance from the main school building.

"Why, good morning to you, ma'am." The stranger spoke with a leisurely US drawl. With his dark moustache, black suit, brocade waistcoat and string tie, he reminded me of Clark Gable as Rhett Butler in *Gone with the Wind*. Scarlett O'Hara would have felt right at home at St Bride's, with its ostentatious historic house and gardens, although

4

our English weather couldn't compete with the southern sunshine at Tara, her family plantation estate.

If the stranger was a belated trick or treater, his choice of costume was unusual. I kept my hand on the doorknob. I wasn't going to let him in without good reason.

"Do you have an appointment, please?"

"Why, thank you, ma'am, I surely do."

He gave a slight bow. Was he mocking me with his elaborate Southern charm?

"And with whom might your appointment be, sir?"

I'm not the kind of English teacher who is a stickler for "whom" in general conversation, but his formal speech was rubbing off on me.

"With Miss Caroline Harnett, your headmistress, if you please. I believe I am right on time."

He patted the pocket in his waistcoat, from which hung a silver watch chain, fastened at the other end to a button. Holding the door open to allow him in, I pointed to the signing-in book on the table beside the sofa.

"If you would be so kind as to write your name in our visitors' book, I'll give you a security badge and tell Miss Harnett you're here."

The stranger bent his head in acknowledgement and produced from his inside jacket pocket an engraved gold fountain pen. He signed his name in copperplate of such a size that it spilled over the edges of the signature box, yet the loops were so tightly closed that I couldn't make out what he'd written.

"Whom shall I say is here for her? I mean, who?"

He added an ornate swirl of self-importance beneath his signature, then gazed up at me in feigned surprise, as

5

if he were a celebrity recognised wherever he went. He straightened up, capped his pen and returned it to its pocket.

"My name is Bunting. Earl Bunting. Thank you kindly."

The gasp that issued from behind the pillar echoed my own surprise. Lord Bunting was the school's Victorian founder. Over a hundred years before, when he'd apparently died without issue, he'd bequeathed his house and grounds to be turned into a boarding school for girls.

I was unsure how to address the stranger. My Lord? Your Excellency? Your Worship? The school library's copy of Debrett's *Peerage* would tell me. We had plenty of titled girls on the roll, but it was school policy not to use those titles in daily life, so I'd never needed to swot up on the etiquette before. For now, I took the easy option.

"Please take a seat, sir, and I'll tell Miss Harnett you're here."

As I marched off to the Headmistress's study, Imogen came pattering after me.

"Now do you believe me, miss? It's the ghost of Lord Bunting, isn't it? Didn't you recognise him?"

The life-size oil painting of the school's founder on the wall of the assembly hall had made him a familiar figure to us all.

Imogen skipped to overtake me, then turned back to face the way we'd come.

"I'm going to the hall now to see if the picture's still there. Lord Bunting might have stepped down from it and turned real. That's the sort of thing that happens at Halloween. I've seen it before."

6

"Really?"

"Yes, in a play my grandma took me to see in the summer holidays. There were lots of songs in it and all the paintings came to life."

"That'll be *Ruddigore*," came a voice behind us – Louisa Humber, the music teacher, was on her way to her classroom. "It's an operetta, Imogen, not a play, by Gilbert and Sullivan."

Imogen shrugged. "Anyhoo, my point is, there's probably now a big empty hole in the painting where Lord Bunting used to be."

Louisa flashed a conspiratorial smile at me.

"Let me know if your ghost bursts into song."

She walked on.

"Off you go then, Imogen." I hoped that when she found the painting intact she would feel reassured. "But be as quick as you can, or you'll be late for your lesson."

"Yes, Miss Lamb."

Not wanting to be late for my lesson either, I hastened down the private corridor to the Headmistress's secluded study and rapped on her door.

"Come in!" came her cheery greeting.

I went in to find Miss Harnett sitting at her desk, contentedly opening her half-term post. Through the bay window behind her lay a neat rose garden, pruned and orderly for the winter. McPhee, her black cat, lay on his side on the window seat, basking in a beam of autumn sunshine, legs stretched out for maximum exposure to the warmth. He's a substantial cat. I mean she. Officially, McPhee is female, like all the teaching staff – one of Miss Harnett's policies for the sake of child protection.

7

"Good morning, my dear. I trust you have had an enjoyable break?"

"Thank you, yes. I felt like one of the girls, going home to see my parents, but it was lovely."

Unlike the girls, I hadn't seen my parents for a few years, due to a disastrous relationship with my controlling ex, Steven, from whom I'd fled to this job and some vestige of security. At last I was starting to make up for lost time. I'd be returning to my parents for the Christmas holidays.

"What can I do for you this morning, my dear?"

The pleasure of being back in the Headmistress's comforting company had almost made me forget the stranger.

"You have a visitor, Miss Harnett. He's waiting in the entrance hall. He claims he has an appointment with you."

She glanced at the large hardback diary that lay open on her desk. Her smile faded.

"Ah, yes, so he does. Please escort him to my study."

She didn't ask his name.

Setting her pile of post aside, she pulled her daybook towards her.

When I'd retraced my steps to the entrance hall, where I found the stranger gazing up at the ornate painted ceiling, I saw him with fresh eyes. His resemblance to the original Lord Bunting was inescapable.

I coughed to attract his attention.

"Miss Harnett will see you now."

I raised a hand to indicate the direction of her study. His reverie interrupted, he stood up and straightened his silk tie.

When we passed the foot of the curving marble staircase that led to the residential part of the school, he patted the final fondly. As he followed me down the oak-panelled corridor to the Headmistress's study, he whistled in admiration.

"It's quite a place we have here," he said in a low voice, as much to himself as to me.

We? I wondered at his choice of pronoun but made no comment.

I knocked on Miss Harnett's door, waited for permission to enter, then held it wide for him to go in.

The Headmistress rose from her desk and crossed the crimson Persian carpet to greet him. Instantly alert, McPhee leapt down from the window seat and followed at Miss Harnett's heels, his tail bushy with hostility.

"Ah, Mr Bunting, I've been expecting you."

Eyes wide, I withdrew and left them to it, just as the bell rang for the first lesson. I would have to wait until morning break to update my colleagues about this mysterious stranger.

2

White Knight

"Bunting. His name's Bunting and he's an Earl."

In the staffroom at break, I blurted out the news with the breathless excitement that often accompanies the girls' more outlandish announcements.

Joe lowered his newspaper.

"I should think he would have to be a member of the nobility to afford such a flash car as that. Or a media mogul or a financier or a film star. Someone loaded, anyway. Have you seen it, Gemma?"

He got up from his habitual armchair and led me to the window, his guiding hand gentle on my shoulder. It felt good to physically connect with him again. Before half term, we'd been on the brink of striking up a romantic relationship, but I was reticent post-Steven. I wasn't going to rush into a new relationship on the rebound.

All the same, I was glad he kept his hand on my shoulder as he pointed to a gleaming white Rolls-Royce on the forecourt.

"Wow!"

I couldn't contain my admiration, although I wasn't surprised at the calibre of the car, given Earl Bunting's expensive tailoring and fancy fountain pen.

Joe grinned. "And get that licence plate!"

I read it aloud.

"BL1 55."

It took me a moment to realise what he meant. Then I shouted across the staffroom.

"Oriana, come and look at this!"

Oriana had just come into the staffroom and was helping herself to a drink from Old Faithful, the dependable but dangerous staffroom coffee machine. Sipping her coffee, she strolled languidly to the window, but the sight of the car perked her up more than any amount of caffeine. She flushed with pleasure.

"BL1 55. Oh, BLISS! That's me! Whose is it? I want it!"

Her eyes gleamed more than the car. Oriana was a pushover for a fancy car at the best of times, so a fancy car with a personalised number plate was bound to appeal.

As a former professional cyclist, Joe was less easily impressed. He preferred two wheels for transport. With an indulgent smile, he shook his head and returned to his armchair, leaving me to fill in the details for her.

By now I knew Oriana well enough to tease her a little.

"What's more, it comes with a title: Earl Bunting. He had an appointment with Hairnet this morning."

Oriana's head jerked back in astonishment.

"Really?"

A title as well as a posh car. She was probably already picturing their wedding. The Rolls-Royce would have made an excellent wedding car.

Judith Gosling, Head of History, came over to join us, clutching her week's post just retrieved from her pigeonhole.

"He can't be the current Lord Bunting, if that's what you're thinking."

Judith is our resident expert on genealogy and the author of a slim book about the school's history.

Oriana turned on Judith crossly.

"Are you sure?"

Judith didn't let Oriana's brusque tone upset her.

"When Miss Harnett asked me to draw up the Bunting family tree for the school website a few years ago, it ended with our founder. Poor Lord Bunting's family tree was fairly coppiced. Like those of so many Victorian parents, his marriage wasn't without issue, but no children survived him. Shame, really. I got the impression he would have been a good father, at least by the standards of his day."

"That's odd. This new Earl Bunting was talking like he owned the place, or at least had a claim to it. Although I did find it strange that he had an American accent."

Judith raised her eyebrows. "Really? The family didn't stray much from the Cotswolds, never mind as far as America. Even with all that wealth at his disposal, Lord Bunting only ever went to London for business meetings about his inventions and for his Parliamentary duties. What sort of American accent was it?"

In my head, I replayed my conversation with the stranger.

"Deep South, I'd say."

Judith tapped her handful of post in thought.

"There was a time when a wealthy British family might have invested in tobacco or sugar or cotton plantations in the Americas and sent a son to run it. But Bunting's was a sparse dynasty. I can't think of anyone in his family who might have done that. In any case, my impression is that he was a decent man who would have had no truck with the slave trade, thank goodness."

"I gather he had no children in any case."

"No known surviving children, at any rate. His only legitimate child to live beyond babyhood died when he was nine, poor little soul."

This was sad news.

"But you should see this fellow, Judith. He is the spitting image of Lord Bunting's portrait, even down to the cut of his clothes and the shape of his moustache. And he did introduce himself as Earl Bunting. Surely he must be some kind of relation."

Judith slipped her post in her bookbag.

"Whether or not he's related makes no difference. Bunting was only a life peer. His title died with him, whether or not he had children. Besides which, he was never an Earl. An Earldom is hereditary. If you're an Earl, you're Earl of somewhere, such as Earl Wendlebury, which would have been Bunting's obvious choice, given how much he loved the place. But, even then, he wouldn't have introduced himself as Earl Wendlebury, nor would you address him as that. You'd say either 'My Lord' or 'Lord Wendlebury.'"

"Like the poet Byron. George Gordon, Lord Byron. That makes sense. I thought it odd that Hairnet called him 'Mr Bunting' and that her infallible curtsey reflex in the presence of nobility didn't kick in."

Joe laughed from behind his newspaper.

"You've been had, Gemma. I bet he's no more an Earl than I am. You know what these Americans are like with names. His mother must have had delusions of grandeur. He probably puts Roman numerals after his name, too – Earl Bunting III or some such – because his forebears lacked the imagination to name him anything different from his father or grandfather. How to quash a child's individuality from birth in one fell blow."

Gazing at the white Rolls-Royce, Oriana sighed like a deflating wedding balloon.

"I'd still like a ride in that car, though."

Reluctantly she tore herself away from the window to return her coffee cup to the trolley.

Joe grinned.

"Nobody's stopping you, Oriana. I bet you can wangle a ride in the Blissmobile if you tell this Bunting guy your name."

Before she could accept the challenge, the staffroom door was flung wide open and Felicity Button, Head of Essential Life Skills, entered bearing a plate of gingerbread stars. She proceeded to tour the room, offering them to us in turn.

Judith was first to help herself.

15

"Eight," said Felicity to Judith, who looked as if it meant something to her.

Felicity held out the plate to me.

"Go on, take a handful while they're warm. Gentler on the teeth this way too. Gingerbread hardens as it cools."

I didn't need to be asked twice, but Oriana, apparently back on her dating diet, declined, and diverted Felicity's attention to Mr Bunting's car.

"Look at this, Felicity. A Rolls-Royce with my name on it."

Felicity went to join her at the window.

"Who gave you that, then? You must have had a successful half-term."

Oriana stiffened.

"Actually, I'm between beaux," was her prim reply, before she weakened and took a biscuit. "Though I'm hoping to meet the owner of that little beauty once Hairnet's done with him."

Felicity stared at the car in thought.

"While you're at it, could you please ask him whether he'll let my car maintenance class have a glimpse under the bonnet? That's my next lesson. A Rolls-Royce would make an interesting change from my Mini. Besides, most of our girls are more likely to drive a big posh car than a hatchback when they grow up."

Miss Button's portfolio is very broad, from cookery to car maintenance, from how to vote to how to fill in a tax return – or a betting slip. I wish I'd had a Miss Button when I was at school.

"What a splendid subject for the last car maintenance lesson of the autumn term," Felicity continued. "For the rest of this term, my classes will be focused on food. Christmas pudding, Christmas cake, brandy butter, mince pies, Stollen, panettone. Yum!"

My hands went involuntarily to my waist. Thanks to school dinners, I'd put on several kilos since joining the staff.

"And we'll get to sample them all, Gemma," said Joe, patting his tummy, enviably taut beneath his tracksuit. "There have to be some perks to this job."

I rather hoped he might prove to be one of mine before the Christmas term was out.

3

The Day of the Dead

"Well, it *is* the Day of the Dead," Imogen was saying as I took my seat at the head of my lunch table in the Trough, the girls' dining room.

"Does that mean we have to hold a funeral?" asked one of her friends.

"Bagsy not me as human sacrifice," said another. "Can't we bury a dead beetle or something instead?"

As I drew in my chair, the girls started to hand round big dishes of a luscious-looking casserole, creamy mashed potatoes and steamed broccoli with toasted almonds. Joe had told me the food was always better following a break. The school cook, Rosemary, must have been in a good mood after a holiday with her husband, Max Security.

I tried not to let the sumptuous spread distract me from my pastoral duties.

"Girls, girls! That's not how the Day of the Dead works at all."

All eyes around our table fixed on me.

"Really, miss?" asked Imogen. "Are you an expert on the Day of the Dead?"

"I'm no expert, but I know a little about it from my RE GCSE. We studied religious rites and rituals around the world, and the Day of the Dead was one of them. It takes place the day after All Saints' Day, so two days after Halloween."

"We know all about Halloween, Miss Lamb," said Grace. The bulging bags of trick or treat bounty they'd brought back after half term proved her point.

"The Day of the Dead is a Mexican tradition," I continued. "It celebrates family and friends who have passed away. There are solemn prayers, but also lots of fun, such as fancy-dress processions, music, dancing, and special food and drink. Shrines are set up with photos and candles to remember lost loved ones. It's a happy occasion really."

Imogen's hand was shaking as she filled my water glass from the jug. "Do the dead come back to life to join in?"

I gave what I hoped was a reassuring smile.

"No, of course not. That's not possible, is it?"

Spooning casserole on to my plate from the dish that Imogen was holding out to me, I chose my words carefully. Many of the girls at St Bride's were half-orphaned, having lost their mothers at least. Motherless pupils received a discount on school fees, as stipulated by Lord Bunting in his will, for reasons best known to himself.

"If you've ever lost anyone – and I know a lot of you have – you'll know you can't help but think about them

20

long after they've gone. Sometimes it feels as if they've never really left you, and as if they're watching over you. You could say they are still with you in spirit, but that's not the same thing as their being ghosts. And there's nothing spooky or scary about that."

The girls remained silent, giving me their full attention, so I carried on.

"After all, we are the product of those who love us and care for us. It's natural they should always feel part of our lives. I lost my grandparents when I was about your age, and I still think about them a lot. Sometimes in my dreams I go to tea with them, as I used to do when I was little, and I wake up peaceful and contented."

The girls had hardly touched their food yet, so I thought I'd better bring this conversation to a close.

"So it's a good, positive thing to have a special day to celebrate them. Mexicans see the Day of the Dead as a day of joy and happiness, just as we see the birthdays of those who are still with us. Now, let's get on with our lunch, please, or you'll have no time to play before next lesson."

The rest of the meal passed without further event, most of the girls deep in thought about what I'd said. I love it when that happens – not the silence, but the feeling that I've made a mark on the girls. Moments like this confirm my impression that I've made the right career choice at last. I have come to understand how Miss Harnett, with decades of such experiences to her credit, cares so passionately about St Bride's. Her dedication is infectious.

* * *

As I crossed the assembly hall to the staffroom for post-lunch coffee, I couldn't help but glance up at Lord Bunting's portrait, just to check he was still there. As ever, Lord Bunting, whose deep brown eyes follow you around the room, smiled at me benignly down his aquiline nose, flanked by high cheekbones. His mouth was lean but wide beneath the neat moustache that arched like a third eyebrow above his thin lips. It was a patrician face, although his title had been bestowed on him as a reward for his most renowned invention, rather than by birthright.

The school community took a vicarious pride in Lord Bunting's chief claim to fame - not the construction of the beautiful house and grounds we now called home, but his standing as a prominent Victorian engineer. He invented a highly effective tunnelling machine that played a major part in the construction of railways throughout the country and even across the former British Empire. He'd also deployed his patented machine to build a series of tunnels on his home turf. A man-sized rabbit warren honeycombed the St Bride's estate, now invaluable for Max Security when patrolling the grounds.

Scrutinising Lord Bunting's portrait, I couldn't help but see the image of our visitor. Yet despite the physical resemblance, there were some significant differences. Earl's lips were straight and unsmiling, and his deep brown eyes lacked the kindly twinkle of his supposed ancestor's.

As I headed for the staffroom, I shivered. The school had not yet returned to its normal temperature after the week's closure for half term. Even its normal temperature was on the chilly side.

The Bursar scuttled behind me, overtaking me just in time to open the staffroom door. We hadn't hit it off when I first joined the school, so when I realised he was holding the door open for me, I was glad to see he wasn't bearing any grudges. I turned to smile at him as I crossed the threshold.

"Thanks, Bursar."

I'd quickly fallen into the quaint school habit of addressing him by his title. Some staff called Miss Harnett 'Headmistress' as well. The tradition had seemed odd at first, but I soon got used to it. Even so, I was glad that the girls called the teachers by their title and surname, or just "miss" for short.

The Bursar followed me across the staffroom to Old Faithful.

"I hear I missed an interesting visitor this morning, Gemma. Thank you for taking care of him. I had no idea he was expected, or I'd have stayed close at hand."

I poured him a cup of coffee and handed it to him before filling a cup for myself.

"It's not like Miss Harnett to forget an appointment," he continued.

I wondered whether he could withstand a little teasing. Carrying the weight of responsibility for managing the school on just one hundred girls' fees, he often looked as if he could do with cheering up. I winked at him.

"Perhaps he is her fancy man and she doesn't want anyone to know."

He nearly choked on his coffee, but not with laughter.

"Goodness, do you think so?"

I was puzzled as to why he looked so upset. I decided to put him out of whatever was causing his misery.

"Actually, she was expecting him. Maybe she wanted to keep his visit confidential, though I don't know why."

He drank the rest of his coffee quickly to restore his equilibrium after the shock.

"Is he still here?" His brow crinkled with worry.

"I don't know, but we can soon find out. Let's see if his car's still on the forecourt."

Before we could reach the window to check, Miss Harnett entered the staffroom with Earl Bunting, McPhee at her heels. The room fell silent.

"Good afternoon, ladies and gentlemen." Her voice sounded formal, and a few notes higher than usual. "We have a visitor. Please welcome to St Bride's, Mr Earl Bunting. He's going to be with us for some time."

4

Musical Chairs

The Bursar took a step forward.

"When you say some time, Headmistress, how long do you mean exactly?"

Miss Harnett glanced at Earl Bunting, checking his reaction before answering. His expression gave nothing away.

"Why, as long as he wishes, Bursar. And the good news is that he's decided to stay on site so that he can spend as much time as possible acquainting himself with the estate to which he has staked his claim."

A slight twitch played beneath the Bursar's right eye.

"Really, Headmistress? I'm not sure of the propriety of allowing a strange man to stay in the same building as the girls."

Miss Harnett was a little too quick to reply.

"I'm sure you have no reason to worry about our guest, Bursar, given his pedigree. It's not as if he'll be sleeping in school."

The Bursar let out a sigh of relief.

"My apologies, Headmistress. I misunderstood. So where will he be sleeping? At The Bluebird?"

The pub in the nearby village of Wendlebury Barrow offers bed and breakfast, a service popular with visiting parents.

Miss Harnett deployed her most charming smile on the Bursar.

"In your house, Bursar. Just as soon as you've had the chance to move your things up to the old butler's quarters in the attic. You'll be fine up there for the time being. If it was good enough for Lord Bunting's butler…"

The Bursar's mouth fell open, but no words came out. He could hardly object without casting doubt on his own suitability to be in close proximity to the girls. Miss Harnett wasn't daft. She had him in a checkmate.

"That's mighty kind of you, sir," said Earl Bunting. "However, it'll be a while before my possessions arrive from the States, so I'd thank you to leave your furniture in place."

Miss Harnett answered on the Bursar's behalf.

"Of course. The butler's old furniture is in his flat, so the Bursar's needs will be well catered for."

As Miss Harnett and Earl Bunting left the room, Mavis got up from her chair and made a beeline for the Bursar.

"Come on, Bursar, I'm free next period. Let me give you a hand with moving your stuff."

Linking her arm through his in solidarity, she led him from the staffroom, leaving the rest of us to ponder on the news.

Joe was first to break the ensuing silence. "That's a slap in the face for poor old Geoffrey. He must feel like he's been demoted."

"At least it keeps Earl Bunting away from the girls at night," I observed. "And no more than a stone's throw from Max, so he shouldn't be able to get into any mischief."

"I wonder why Earl wants to stay in school anyway?" said Felicity.

"His supposed family connection?" said Judith. "Which wouldn't seem unreasonable. Except I'm unsure where he fits in to the family tree. At least, the legitimate part of it. There is always the possibility that Lord Bunting fathered children outside of his marriage."

"So, what do you propose to do about it?" snapped Oriana. "Run a DNA test? I can't see Hairnet giving you permission to open up Lord Bunting's mausoleum to get a sample for comparison. Besides, I think you're all too cynical for words. With all the genes in the world, the chance of someone unrelated turning up out of the blue with such an unmistakeable resemblance to our founder is miniscule. Who's to say Lord Bunting didn't have a son or daughter born out of wedlock to keep his genes from extinction?"

She flushed and her eyes widened.

"Not that there's anything wrong with that these days," said Joe. Joe, the Bursar and I were the only staff members to know that Oriana was Miss Harnett's illegitimate daughter.

"It would have to have been a son to continue the family name," observed the ever-practical Judith. "Let me see what I can find out. I've still got my research notes from the family tree project."

The bell rang for the next lesson and we filed out of the staffroom, heading for the classroom courtyard. I strolled across the quad with Felicity, who had since lunch changed out of her chef's whites and harlequin apron into royal blue mechanic's overalls.

"What did you think of our visitor?" she asked me on the way.

I thought for a moment.

"I don't trust him. He seems a bit smarmy to me."

Felicity mimicked his American accent: "Maybe you're not used to such divine Southern manners, honey."

I grinned. "Anyone can talk like that if they try. It doesn't make them a gentleman, or a relative of one. Besides, how come he is so very similar to the man he claims to be his ancestor? He looks as if he has a hundred per cent of Lord Bunting's genes, yet he's many generations removed. I don't need to be Head of Science to know that with every generation, Lord Bunting's genes will have been diluted by 50%, the other half coming from each descendant's other parent. Earl Bunting's percentage of the original must be in single figures."

Felicity nodded. "It's just like homeopathy. Or baking sourdough bread from a starter batch. By the time you're on your sixth mix, there's hardly any of the original left at all."

I love sourdough bread. I hoped it was on the girls' cookery curriculum this term.

Oriana caught up with us, smiling beatifically.

"All sorted. He's taking me out in his car on my next afternoon off."

I covered my mouth with my hand to hide my smile.

"You haven't wasted any time."

She shrugged. "Well, why not? I've always thought Lord Bunting looked rather dashing. I never thought I'd have the chance to go on a date with him, though. Oh, and Felicity, he said you can take your girls out to check under the hood this afternoon, if you like. The rest of the car will be locked. How generous he is!"

And how fickle you are, I thought, mentally correcting hood to bonnet. Oriana has chameleon tendencies when she's dating, echoing her latest boyfriend's behaviour.

Felicity turned off into her mechanics' workshop, and I lingered outside Oriana's classroom to finish our conversation, the girls filing past us for their next lesson.

"But honestly, don't you find him a bit odd, Oriana? I could understand it if he'd inherited a few distinguishing family features – the aquiline nose or elegant cheekbones, perhaps – but not the whole thing, down to the cut of his moustache. You, of all people, and Joe, as our resident masters of disguise, should know better than to set such store by appearances alone."

Oriana was constantly giving herself a complete makeover to suit her target man of the moment. When I'd first met her, she'd been sporting an Egyptian look, her sights set on the widowed father of Cleo, a pupil from Cairo. As for Joe, growing his hair out of the aerodynamic close crop he'd favoured when cycling competitively and dressing in women's sports gear had become a surprisingly successful disguise.

"Oh, don't be so stuffy, Gemma. You're so unromantic. Hairnet has everything in hand. She's calling an emergency governors' meeting tomorrow to check his authenticity. It'll make a nice change for them to put their legal knowledge to good use."

Given the average age of our ancient governors, I wasn't sure how helpful this would be.

5

All in the Family

When Oriana drifted into the staffroom for coffee after supper, she had a certain glow about her, and it wasn't down to the delicious chicken curry we'd just eaten.

"Where were you at afternoon break?" I asked, trying not to sound accusing. "I fielded a phone call for you from the organiser of some inter-school maths competition, but I couldn't find you anywhere."

It is notoriously difficult to catch staff on the phone during the school day, so callers usually book appointments to speak to teachers in their free time.

Oriana waved a hand dismissively as she headed for Old Faithful.

"Sorry, Gemma, I'd forgotten I'd told that woman to call me today." She poured a conciliatory cup for me too. "Blame Hairnet. She asked me to take Earl Bunting on a tour of the grounds. Although once we got going, he said he hardly needed showing round – it was all coming back to him, like muscle memory across the generations."

That seemed a bit rich. How gullible did he think Oriana was? Hoping to extract more inside information about him, I was careful not to make her clam up. I tried to think of something positive to say about their arrangement.

I kept my voice light and casual. "You had a beautiful afternoon for it." After lunch, the sun had broken through the grey blanket of cloud for half an hour, making the damp lawns and foliage sparkle. "What did he make of the mausoleum?"

The mausoleum is a small stone building in the grounds, housing the tomb of Lord Bunting. His memorial plinth bears a startlingly lifelike marble effigy, which looks as if he's just taken a nap beneath a layer of cream paint. Beside it, a twin plinth intended for his wife remains empty.

Oriana helped herself to a refill, after offering one to me, which I declined for fear of staying awake all night.

"Oh, I didn't take him in there. He said he's not that bothered about really old stuff."

"But it's the resting place of his ancestor. Surely he'd like to see it for sentimental family reasons?"

She wrinkled her nose.

"It's unhealthy to dwell too much on the dead."

Her mother didn't think so. She often enjoyed the seclusion of the place, reclining on the empty plinth to channel inspiration from the school's benefactor. However, as Oriana had suffered an unpleasant incident in the mausoleum during the first half of term, she must

32

have been relieved not to have had to enter the building again.

"So, did you find out why he's here?"

Before she could answer, the door swung open to admit the Bursar, looking glum. Abandoning Oriana, I went over to try to cheer him up.

"Hey, Bursar, I was chatting with Joe and Mavis after lunch and we came up with all sorts of conspiracy theories – that Earl Bunting might be an undercover school inspector, or a brazen burglar casing the joint. What do you reckon?"

The Bursar, not amused, slumped down in Joe's favourite armchair. I doubted the butler's flat, disused for decades, had any such comfy seats to offer him.

"What do I know?" he sighed. "Miss Harnett's going to tell you the governors' verdict after their meeting tomorrow. In the meantime, her instructions are that we're to treat him like one of the family."

"Can we choose which family?" asked Mavis. "Like the Simpsons? Or the Kray twins?"

Oriana returned her empty cup to the trolley. Before heading for the door, she paused beside me.

"I don't know why you're being so hostile, Gemma. Earl Bunting is a perfectly nice man. Look how he loaned his car to Felicity for her grease monkey class this afternoon. He's an utter gentleman."

Then she swept out of the room.

The ensuing silence was broken by a knock at the door. I got up to see who it was, letting the Bursar enjoy some comfort while he could.

33

An unkempt little blonde girl in the youngest class gazed up at me, wide-eyed.

"Have you any matches, please, Miss Lamb?"

"Matches? No, I'm afraid not. Even if I did, I shouldn't be lending them to you. Whatever do you need matches for?"

The little girl twisted the hem of her school skirt in her hands.

"Nothing naughty, Miss Lamb. We just want to light some candles."

"Birthday cake candles are only allowed in the dining room at suppertime, for reasons of health and safety. If someone has a cake, we should have lit its candles then."

She wrapped one leg round the other.

"Not exactly, Miss Lamb. In fact, quite the opposite."

She took a moment to seek the right words, then gave up.

"Come with me, miss, and I'll show you. It's easier."

I followed her to the assembly hall, where we found a semi-circle of the younger pupils cross-legged on the floor beneath Lord Bunting's portrait. In front of it they'd arrayed an assortment of greenery filched from the gardens, some dishes of sweets from their Halloween swag, and a dozen birthday cake candles stuck into a bath sponge in the absence of a cake.

"You see, miss, we just wanted to light some Day of Death candles for Lord Bunting."

Imogen put her hand up to speak.

"Miss Lamb, we're just doing what you said to do at lunchtime: honouring the dead. Especially as he's come back to life today. Do you think he'll disappear at midnight, like Cinderella?"

Another girl corrected her. "No, silly, Cinderella didn't disappear, she just turned back into a pumpkin. I mean, her coach did. But perhaps his clothes will turn back into rags, like Cinderella's ballgown."

Just then, Earl Bunting emerged from the library and strode towards us, stopping when he saw the girls' display. He pointed accusingly at the bath sponge full of candles.

"For gosh sakes, what are you crazy kids up to? Surely you're not thinking of starting a fire, right under that valuable old picture? It has to be worth thousands of bucks. I hope it's well insured." He turned to me, as if somehow this was all my fault. "Now, lookee here, Miss Pony —"

"Miss Lamb," chorused the girls.

He carried on as if they hadn't spoken.

"What kind of discipline do you maintain in this place? Shouldn't these kids be in bed by now instead of wandering the place like this?"

One of the girls began to cry.

Imogen scrambled to her feet and folded her arms across her chest.

"You're not at all how I thought you would be, Your Lordship. I thought you'd be kind and nice, like you are in your picture." She put a comforting arm around her sobbing friend. "This is such a disappointment. I think we'll take our stuff up to our dorm, shall we, guys?"

Her friends assented, gathering up their props in their skirts and slinking off, muttering. Earl Bunting and I watched them go.

35

As soon as they were out of earshot, I turned to him, my hands on my hips.

"That was rather uncalled for, Mr Bunting. In future, please leave the management of the girls to us. You may be a guest of the school, but you're not a member of staff. You are not responsible for the girls' discipline. That's the job of the Headmistress and the teachers."

I stalked off before he could reply. Only when I reached my flat did it occur to me that his intention might be to join the payroll. In what capacity, I couldn't imagine.

6

The Cuckoo in the Nest

The day after Earl Bunting met the governors, Miss Harnett called a meeting of the entire school staff, both teaching and non-teaching. Staff meetings were usually only for teachers. When it became apparent that everyone on the payroll was invited, leaving the sixth form in sole charge of the girls, I knew the news must be momentous.

We gathered in Felicity's classroom, where a tray of oven-warm mince pies awaited us, along with several pots of tea.

"Sugaring the pill," murmured Mavis, taking a seat next to me.

Earl Bunting quietly positioned himself at the back of the classroom, without speaking or engaging with any of us in any way. He even refused refreshments. Just before Miss Harnett started to speak, he assumed the precise stance of Lord Bunting in his portrait. To Miss Harnett, looking straight at him, the effect must have been unnerving.

"Now, my dears," she began, "I'm sure you're all eager to hear the interesting news about our visitor."

She panned the room with a self-conscious smile.

"The good news is that we now have the chance to meet a descendant of our beloved founder, Lord Bunting. What a treat for us all! And not only is Earl Bunting a direct descendant of our founder, but he is also his long-lost heir."

She paused to allow her announcement to sink in.

"As some of you already know, for some years the house and grounds have been under my guardianship."

"Ownership," the Bursar corrected her. "Your ownership."

Miss Harnett gave a slight shake of her head.

"But I now realise I could only have held the St Bride's estate in trust for the rightful heir, should he or she ever make themselves known."

A murmur of concern rippled around the room as she continued speaking.

"There was, nearly thirty years ago, an exchange that the governors, the Bursar and I all thought was entirely legal."

It was common knowledge that Miss Harnett had bought St Bride's for a token sum of one pound sterling, on condition that she maintain both the school and the estate. Only the Bursar, Joe, Oriana and I knew the full details of the exchange. This arrangement was made to compensate her for the chair of governors' bad behaviour towards her. He had fathered Oriana, despite being married and having no intention of leaving his wealthy wife for Miss Harnett, nor of wrecking his career as chief executive of a large corporation. Gifting her the Bunting estate was meant to offer both her and her unborn child lifelong security.

Oriana, sitting on my other side, turned pale.

"Or rather, we thought it was legal, but only because we were under the illusion that Lord Bunting had no heir. Ever since, I have fulfilled all the obligations that might be expected of the owner of this marvellous property. The governors assure me that I have sustained and even added to its value during my stewardship. But now that we have discovered Lord Bunting does have a living heir, I can pass the estate to its rightful owner with a clear conscience."

Her audience was getting fidgety. We all glanced around the room to assess our colleagues' reactions.

Earl smirked at us.

"Let me assure any doubters among you that I have the paperwork to prove my descent. The will, birth certificates, a historic journal – all indisputable evidence."

Miss Harnett acknowledged his interruption with a tight smile.

"However, there is no need for any of you to be alarmed, my dears. To all intents and purposes, life at St Bride's School will be unaffected by the change of ownership. This historic estate will remain home to our school. To our pupils and their parents, there will be no tangible difference."

"Cut to the chase," Mavis murmured.

Miss Harnett did not hear her.

"As I now return ownership to the family, we remain under Bunting's ever-watchful eye."

Was she alluding to the founder's portrait or to our visitor?

"So, in the presence of you all as witnesses, I call upon you now –"

Joe leaned forward to whisper over my shoulder, "Don't tell me she's going to marry him?"

Miss Harnett signalled to Earl Bunting to join her at the front of the room. He loped up the aisle between the rows of cookery tables, milking the moment's dramatic effect. I wondered whether he'd ever done any amateur dramatics. On reaching Miss Harnett, he slipped his hand into his pocket. Then with the flourish of a conjuror producing an egg from behind an onlooker's ear, he pulled out a one-pound coin and held it aloft between thumb and forefinger, little finger raised in mock elegance.

"It is my pleasure to return your stake, ma'am," he announced.

Miss Harnett held out her hand and he dropped the coin into her palm. As she stared at it, I thought of Jack's mother receiving five beans in return for her prize cow. Then she regained her composure.

"And now we have formally completed our transaction, Mr Bunting would like to say a few words."

She stepped aside to give him centre stage and went to sit in the teacher's chair at the desk in the corner of the room.

Earl Bunting struck a confident pose, legs splayed, one thumb in his waistcoat pocket, as if touching his pocket watch for luck. Perhaps the watch had been passed down from his ancestor, who sported a similar watch chain in his portrait.

For a moment he surveyed our faces in silence, gauging our expressions before deciding how to pitch for our sympathies.

"Why the glum faces, my friends? I thought we were getting along swell. Didn't you hear what your Headmistress just said? My ownership of the Saint –" he always said the word in full American-style, rather than the more British "snt" – "Bride's estate is just a technicality. It won't make any difference to you as you go about your daily duties. Why, you'll hardly know I'm here, when I am here. You see, although this is my ancestral home, I don't have my forebear's desire to be here 24/7/365. I'm a city boy, who needs a regular fix of the bright lights, the sounds, the smell of a city that never sleeps."

Mavis leaned towards me to whisper, "That's New York. I thought he hailed from the Deep South?"

If Earl Bunting heard her comment, he chose to ignore it.

"So it's business as usual for you guys. I'll make myself scarce, don't you worry. Besides, your delightful Headmistress tells me that having a member of the Bunting lineage in charge will add value in the eyes of the parents. It's real classy. The only way is up, guys."

Mavis leaned into me again.

"No-one with any real class would ever dream of describing himself as classy. Pleb."

As Earl Bunting finished speaking, fidgety noises began to ripple across the room, reminiscent of the girls when they know the end-of-lesson bell is due.

41

Miss Harnett returned to Earl's side and clapped her hands for silence.

"And now, back to work, my chickens." She waved us away with both hands. "And have a pleasant and productive afternoon."

She left the room before us, Bunting at her heels, bearing the smuggest grin I've ever seen.

Mavis covered her face with her hands.

"Is the woman barking mad?"

Max got up to lean over our seats, one hand on Mavis's shoulder, the other on mine.

"Affirmative. But let's look on the bright side. He could have said he'd close the school and chuck us all out. At least you've still got your jobs and your flats. But never fear, folks. Max Security smells a rat – and it wears a waistcoat with a pocket watch. I'm going to make a few enquiries. Maybe I can rustle up something untoward in his past that makes him unfit to be here. I might even be able to scupper his claim on the estate."

"Ever the optimist," I said, trying to sound pleased.

Pulling a tissue from her pocket to wipe her eyes, Mavis followed the rest of the staff as they filed out of the room. Only Oriana, Joe and I hung back. Oriana remained motionless in her chair, and I went over to check she was OK. As I approached, she leapt to her feet so abruptly that her chair went tumbling backwards.

"It's all right for you two," she cried. "But I've just lost my inheritance."

With that, she fled the room.

7

Caught in the Web

"I suppose I could just marry him."

Oriana's left thumb rubbed her empty ring finger. It had taken her less than a day to bounce back with a plan.

The three of us were alone in the staffroom after lunch. Joe sat back in his usual armchair, stretching out his long legs.

"Does Earl Bunting get any say in the matter?"

She swatted the top of his head with her class register.

"What else am I meant to do to secure my right – and my mother's – to stay here? Besides, I've always fancied the idea of being Lady Bunting."

I exchanged glances with Joe. He was just opening his mouth to offer some suggestions when the staffroom door swung open to silence him.

In bounded Max, who gestured to me to join him for a private discussion in a corner of the room.

"No joy on the Child Protection Register." Max was the school's Child Protection Officer, responsible for checking all staff's backgrounds. "Or rather, no incrimination yet. Bunting's name's not on there, so we can't bust him on that basis."

Of course, no-one wanted him to be guilty of this hideous kind of crime, but at least it would have allowed us to eject him from the school without more ado.

"Nothing else dodgy in his background?"

He shook his head.

"Nothing yet, but I'll keep trying. I'm going to target the US Inland Revenue Service next. Maybe he's running away from a big unpaid tax bill in his home country. They often catch slippery Mafia members that way, you know."

His eyes glazed over as he fantasised about the prospect. I had nothing tangible to offer him but had to work with what I did have: anecdotal feedback.

"Some of the younger girls claim he spooks them, but that's probably just a hangover from Halloween," I told him. "They were also offended by how abrupt he was on Monday night when he saw them planning to light candles beneath Lord Bunting's portrait in the hall."

Max perked up.

"What were they doing, making sacrifices?"

I folded my arms.

"Oh, Max, don't let the girls hear you say that. They've got vivid enough imaginations without you putting more mad ideas into their minds."

Max's head jerked in the direction of the door, his nose twitching like a hound scenting its quarry.

"Speak of the devil," he said, as who should come striding into the staffroom but Earl Bunting.

"Ah, Miss Lump," he cried, ignoring the others in the room and stepping in between Max and me. "Can you spare me ten minutes?"

I could, but I didn't want to.

"I don't know. I don't want to be late for my next lesson."

He glanced at the clock over the door.

"You've plenty of time. Now come this way."

Enticing me with a bent forefinger, he reminded me of the witch in the gingerbread house in an old *Hansel and Gretel* picture book I'd had as a child.

I followed him out of the staffroom and down the corridor into the empty dining room. I supposed he wanted to speak to me without being overheard. Uncomfortable at being alone with him, I was glad of the large windows overlooking the gardens, where some of the younger girls were playing on the lawns. I hoped they'd be close enough to bear witness if he tried anything on. Then I remembered Max had a surveillance camera on the ceiling. I tried not to look at it, not wanting to give the game away to Earl.

He pulled out a couple of dining chairs and beckoned me to sit beside him.

"Say, Miss Lamp, you're new here, aren't you?"

I nodded, wary of speaking.

"Then I guess you've been learning the ropes. There are a few things that puzzle me here, and I was hoping you could explain them."

I hesitated.

"Perhaps you should be talking to someone with more experience, to a longer-serving member of staff. Like Oriana Bliss, for example."

I thought I might as well steer him in her direction.

The corners of his lips twitched.

"I don't think so, missy. You see, I need some unbiased advice from someone who is still new enough to be objective."

I stayed silent, wondering where this was leading.

"Not like Joe, now. Tell me what you know about Joe."

My pulse speeded up. Was he on to Joe's secret identity?

"What's his game, now? Is he bi? Trans? Cross-dressing? Because you can't fool me – I know he is a man, for all that the girls call him Miss."

To play for time, I went to fetch a glass of water from the serving hatch and brought him one too. I set the glasses down on the table and resumed my seat before answering.

"I'm afraid I can't tell you, but Joe is here with the Headmistress's blessing, and it's between the two of them."

Earl took a sip of water and sighed.

"You're sharp, Miss Lamp. I can see I'm not going to get much out of you. I thought you might be a little more forthcoming, given your predecessor's behaviour."

"My predecessor?" Now he'd got me. I couldn't help but be intrigued. The previous Head of English had been sacked for some misdemeanour, but I had yet to discover what this was. "How do you know my predecessor? I thought you'd never been to St Bride's before."

He leaned one elbow on the table and rested his chin on his hand.

"Have you never heard of social media, Miss Lamp?"

I sensed he was using my title ironically, rather than out of respect. "A guy doesn't have to be in the same latitude and longitude to hook up with a girl anymore."

I gasped.

"You mean she was a hooker?"

He let out a roar of laughter and slapped his thigh hard. I was glad it wasn't my thigh.

"Bless you, no, honey. It was she who hooked me up with the school. She shared two photos of my ancestor on social media, one of his portrait and the other of his effigy in the mausoleum. She wanted to demonstrate to her students how far a post might go. It's a common enough trick among school staff. Pretty thrilling to a bunch of kids stuck in the middle of nowhere like this to find their post liked by an American gentleman like me, huh?"

"Now hang on a minute." I couldn't let him get away with being so patronising. "Some of these girls have a social circle and a geographical range to rival minor royalty. They're not going to be so easily impressed."

Indeed, some of the girls from overseas actually were minor royalty, but I wasn't going to tell him that.

He sat back, a satisfied smile spreading over his lean features. I stared at the moustache levitating above his thin lips like a sinister caterpillar. Odd that the same shaped moustache looked dashing on Lord Bunting.

"Now is that so, darling?" I bridled at the inappropriate endearment. "Maybe that explains why the girls feel such

47

a connection with me, what with my noble bloodline and all."

Noble bloodline, my eye. Didn't he realise Lord Bunting's peerage wasn't hereditary?

"We had quite a correspondence going, your predecessor and I, for a while. She wrote long emails telling me all about the school. She even invited me over."

"But how did she know where to find you? Until you arrived on Monday, none of us had any idea that you existed."

He raised his eyebrows teasingly.

"Why no, we made each other's acquaintance only recently when a friend of mine forwarded one of her Twitter posts to me. It had already been retweeted thousands of times, as so often happens when a teacher makes an appeal for shares for educational purposes. He remarked upon the likeness between the portrait and myself."

Again, he assumed the pose that Lord Bunting held in the portrait. It was startlingly accurate. He must have been practising.

"So, what's a gentleman to do but respond to a lady's appeal? I thought she and her students would get a kick out of seeing my picture, and I photoshopped a snap of Lord Bunting and me together in the frame. I matched his outfit as closely as I could and thinned my moustache to resemble his, and hey presto, we're twins. Hashtag twopeasinapod."

I had to agree.

"So began a correspondence, and all was fine and dandy till your Miss Harnett got wind of our liaison. For some reason, she went crazy ape bananas. Next thing I knew, your predecessor's social media accounts disappeared into the ether, and poof! So had she."

He raised his hands in the air, fingers fluttering away to his sides. I had always wondered why my predecessor had been sacked. It irked me now that Earl was the one to tell me the reason: for betraying the girls' privacy and thus putting their security at risk. No wonder Miss Harnett had resorted to such a drastic measure.

Now I wondered whether Earl was hinting he could get me sacked too, if I didn't cooperate. But I'd had enough of controlling men. I wasn't about to let Earl boss me around.

"I can't pretend I wasn't a little concerned at her disappearance," he continued. "She seemed like a mighty fine woman and I looked upon her as a friend. It crossed my mind that the school might have closed, but its website was still live and recruiting new students. So I thought I'd cross the pond for a vacation to see my twin's portrait in real life. I thought it might be a gas, you know?"

He paused for breath.

"Then I showed my mom the photo, and you know what? She revealed that there truly was a historic family connection between us."

That confused me.

"You mean you didn't know until then you were related to Lord Bunting?"

He raised his hands in mock surrender.

"Honey, I thought my family were pure and simple Americans. Honest injun, I'd never traced my family tree or known anyone older than my grandmother. I never was much interested in history. Then my momma spilled the beans."

"Go on."

"Several generations back, a young woman named Mary O'Flaherty fled the old country to take her chances the other side of the pond. She had little baggage to bring with her, except one secret smuggled deep inside her: the illegitimate baby of Lord Bunting. She was fleeing to avoid hurting Lord Bunting's wife, who had suffered a terrible bereavement on losing her only son to survive infancy. He was just nine years old.

"When Mary's son was born, she kept the name of his father a secret and hid her journal of her romance with Lord Bunting. Only on her deathbed did she pass it on to her son, swearing him to secrecy for the sake of her reputation. He gave the diary to his son, who passed it on to his daughter, and so on, right down to my momma. Now Momma intended to follow the family tradition of keeping the secret lifelong, and only when I showed her Lord Bunting's portrait, thinking to amuse, did she break down and tell me the truth. I have to say to you, Miss Lame, I come from mighty proud stock, where being born out of wedlock is still a source of shame, and the salacious details in Mary's very intimate journal were hardly the kind of material a mother wants to share with her children and grandchildren."

By now I was hanging on his every word, but there was one detail he hadn't explained.

"So how come your last name is Bunting?"

He smiled.

50

"Once I knew the secret family history, I decided it was time to shake off the old mantle of shame and celebrate the family heritage. I'm a terrible liar, Miss Lamb. It's a born weakness, I just can't dissemble. The first name I didn't have to change. That was the name I was baptised with, just like my late father before me and his father before him, and I am proud to continue our family tradition."

Earl Bunting III, as Joe had quipped. Well, Earl Something III, anyway.

"So then just recently to honour my ancient forebear, I decided to change my last name to Bunting in law. Once I'd fixed up all the paperwork, I applied for a new passport, so I could hop right on over to visit, and, well, here I am."

To visit? Perhaps he wasn't planning to stay long after all.

"You'll have so much to tell your mother when you see her. She must be missing you. When is your flight back?"

He fixed me with Lord Bunting's eyes.

"Oh, but honey, weren't you listening to your Headmistress like a good girl yesterday? What's that quaint saying over here? An Englishman's home is his castle? Well, in this case, this castle is my home."

It wasn't a castle, it was a Victorian mansion, but Earl didn't appear to know the difference.

"I'm staying right here at St Bride's to secure my rightful claim, just like my great-something-grandmother Mary O'Flaherty should have done all those years ago."

I sat bolt upright.

51

"But hang on, Miss Harnett said the school would continue as before. She said your ownership is just a technicality."

He pushed back his chair, got to his feet and dusted down his lapels.

"Miss Harnett may call the shots to you, honey, but she sure ain't my Headmistress."

I wasn't prepared to listen to him disrespect the woman who had been so kind to me, to my colleagues and to the girls. Whatever his parentage, she was worth a hundred of him.

"Just a minute there, Earl." I stood up too, reaching across the table and grabbing his sleeve to delay his departure. "What proof do you have of your supposed right to the estate? How do we know you're not just spinning a yarn? You've said yourself that the internet led you here. But the internet isn't infallible. For all we know, you could be any old conman. There's an abundant supply online."

He shook his sleeve free of my grasp. Then with his head on one side, he pointed both forefingers at his cheekbones.

"As Head of English, will you take me to task for using a cliché when I say my face is my fortune? Surely it's enough proof in itself?"

I peered at his face, hoping to find evidence of cosmetic surgery, but there were no scars.

"If you still don't believe me, come out to my automobile right now and I'll show you Mary O'Flaherty's journal." He gave me a lascivious leer. "I just hope you're broad-minded, honey."

Although the last thing I wanted to see was proof of his claim, it was an offer I couldn't refuse.

8

Mud Sticks

"My automobile! My beautiful automobile!"

As soon as we opened the front door, it was obvious that something dreadful had happened to Earl Bunting's car. Instead of the Rolls-Royce, gleaming white and shiny as an igloo, a rust-brown mess stood adrift in a sea of muck.

The effect was not caused by actual rust, but by a mass of autumn leaves glued liberally to the paintwork with treacle-coloured mud. It was a car's equivalent of being tarred and feathered.

Earl paled, motionless beneath the porch, speechless for once. Then the colour began to flood back to his cheeks, and by the time he stormed over to inspect the vehicle at close range, his face was crimson with rage.

"Miss Lame, whichever girls committed such sabotage on my vehicle –" he gave the word three syllables, ve-hi-cle "– I hope you will punish them severely."

55

He turned to me so accusingly that for a moment, I thought he assumed I was a co-conspirator.

I covered my smile with my hands and spoke through my fingers.

"Don't worry, I'll find out who did it and make them wash it all off."

He waved a clenched fist.

"Simply undoing what they've done is hardly a punishment. I demand a formal apology."

My heart sank. Ever since I'd joined the school, the girls had behaved well for me. I'd not had to go beyond a gentle reprimand for a late piece of prep or for talking in a silent study period. I didn't want to lose their trust or respect by appearing to be in league with a bully. What would Miss Harnett do in such circumstances?

Putting Mary O'Flaherty's journal out of my mind, I had no choice but to assure him that I'd get on the case straight away.

* * *

I found the culprits gathered together in their dormitory's bathroom which was now splattered in as much mud as they were. It was the same group Earl had admonished about the Day of the Dead shrine to Lord Bunting. So engrossed were they in their pursuit of cleanliness that it took them a while to notice me standing in the doorway.

When I had cleared my throat to attract their attention, they all shrieked at being caught mud-handed.

"There's no point trying to wash the mud off yourselves yet," I told them. "Because first you're to go

56

straight back out to the forecourt and clean Mr Bunting's car until it's spotless."

One of the girls put up her hand for permission to speak, her eyes full of tears.

"But we've got Miss Brook next lesson and she'll go nuclear if we turn up covered in mud."

I could well imagine she might.

"Perhaps you should have thought of that before you decided to spend your lunchtime playing mud pies with Mr Bunting's very expensive car. And when you've finished, you must write a letter of apology. Please bring it to the staffroom and ask someone to put it in his pigeonhole."

It irked me that Earl had already been allocated a named pigeonhole, as if he were a member of staff.

"Yes, Miss Lamb," they chorused, drying their hands with mud-streaked towels.

I stood back as they trooped past me, shoulders sagging, to do as I'd said. Then the last in the line turned round, wide-eyed, to ask a question.

"What if we're late for Miss Brook's lesson? We'll never get it all done by the time the bell goes."

"Don't worry, I'll make it right with Miss Brook." There was no need to tell them that I thought she'd be delighted at the news.

"Righto. Thanks, miss."

The child slunk away to catch up with her friends.

After wiping as much mud as I could from the hand basins – the girls could clean the rest of the surfaces after lessons – I returned to the staffroom in search of Mavis Brook. On arrival, I found all the staff crowded on to the long window seat, enjoying the spectacle of a bevy of girls cleaning Earl's vandalised car. It seemed the staff were getting as much pleasure from the sight of the mucky vehicle as from the girls' antics.

Already the girls seemed less downhearted, taking time out from their task to stick muddy leaves on each other's backs. A couple of them were assembling the mud and leaves removed from the car into a snowman shape in the empty parking space beside it. I was glad their punishment hadn't broken their spirit. Shaped by Miss Harnett's philosophy, these young things would deal with whatever life threw at them, including the Earl Buntings of this world.

I squeezed in between Mavis and Oriana to watch the girls' progress.

"That's the downside of a white car," Felicity said with a twinkle in her eye. "It's a magnet for every bit of mud on the road."

Oriana, the only one of us not smiling, stepped back from the throng.

"Well, I think it's too silly for words. Mindless desecration of a prestige car."

She seized her pile of books from the table and strode off early for her next lesson.

Mavis looked at the wall clock.

"We've ages yet, folks."

That reminded me.

"You've got more time than the rest of us, Mavis, because all those girls are due with you next lesson. I told them I'd warn you they'd be late. Will you give them detention?"

Mavis looked at me askance.

"Goodness, no. This is far too entertaining. I'm tempted to give them each a house point for ingenuity. I might as well relax and enjoy the spectacle now."

She went to help herself to another coffee.

Hazel Taylor, the art teacher, was taking photos on her mobile phone.

"That's quite an installation they've made there. I'd have liked to preserve it until the next rainfall if I didn't think it would upset that American blighter."

She took one last shot before collecting her register from her pigeonhole, ready for class. One by one the other staff followed suit, until only Mavis, Joe and I remained at the window.

"Come on, Gemma," said Joe, patting me amiably on the shoulder. "I'm going your way now. I've got a theory lesson with the Year 11s next. Like to walk across to the quad with me?"

"Sure."

As we turned into the corridor, I took the opportunity to seek his advice.

"Can I be sure Mavis won't give them a detention?"

He laughed.

"Not her. If she could have got away with it, she'd have been out there with them. Before you came into the staffroom just now, she was all for uprooting a tree and chucking it on top of the car roof."

* * *

After lessons, I was alone in the staffroom marking some Year 9 poetry critiques when there came a knock at the door. When I went to open it, Imogen and two of her partners in crime were huddled together, each holding a corner of a small white envelope bearing brown fingerprints. The envelope was addressed in capital letters to "URL BUNTING". That would teach him to give himself such airs and graces.

"We're very sorry, Miss Lamb, we won't do it again," said Imogen.

"That's OK, girls. Just learn from the experience, put it behind you and move on."

Perhaps I erred too far on the side of sympathy, because they all began justifying their misdemeanour.

"But he was so mean to us –"

"He disrespected Lord Bunting –"

"He disrespected us –"

I held up my hands for silence.

"Remember, girls, I was there. I heard exactly what he said to you, and I can understand why you were upset. But that doesn't mean I'm condoning your response. I think you've got off very lightly, considering what a mess you made of his beautiful car. Which, by the way, I shall now go and inspect, and if it's not fully restored to its former pristine condition, I'll be calling you all out there again after supper to finish it off."

"We did our best, miss, we really did," said Imogen.

"I believe you. Now, run along and get ready for supper. And no more silly pranks."

"Yes, miss."

"Yes, Miss Lamb."

"We will."

Although I didn't want to leave the cosy warmth of the staffroom on this chilly evening, I thought I'd better keep my word to the girls, so I fetched my coat and scarf from my flat and set out into the darkening forecourt.

9

Caught on Camera

The advantage of making a snowman out of mud and leaves is that he will not melt. I wondered what Earl Bunting would make of the girls' sculpture beside his car, but I didn't care, provided they'd done a good job of the clean-up.

I walked around the Rolls-Royce to check that every last speck of mud had been removed. Doing a second circuit, I checked the wheels. The hub caps were as spotless as the bodywork. Headlights, wing mirrors, rear lights – all were immaculate. Then I caught sight of the front licence plate. Although clear of leaves, it was spattered with mud and still bore witness to one detail of the attack that I hadn't noticed before. Some young wag had taken a black whiteboard marker and, with the strategic application of a few straight lines, turned the registration number from "BL1 55" into "BOSSY". I sniggered, then looked around to check no-one had heard me.

I shrieked in alarm when I saw a man behind me, but it was only Max Security, arriving with characteristic stealth. A khaki parka over his usual camouflage cargo trousers, he trudged towards me with a box of outdoor fairy lights under his arm.

"Just rigging up the lighting for tonight's bonfire party." He nodded at the car. "Hope it wasn't you who cleared all that muck off His Lordship's Roller."

"Not likely! I made the girls do it. I'm just checking their handiwork."

He pointed to the front licence plate.

"They missed a bit."

I grinned.

"I know. I was just contemplating whether to leave it like that to teach him a lesson."

Max didn't say a word to discourage me, but my conscience took over.

"But I'd better not wind him up any further. He's bad enough in his natural state."

I delved into my book bag to pull out a packet of tissues and a little bottle of antibacterial hand gel.

"This should do the trick."

Max watched me wipe the licence plate clean. When I tackled the edges, to my surprise, something white came off along with the mud.

"That's weird." I held the tissue up to show him. "It looks like he's whitewashed out the line of lettering at the top of the plate."

Max shrugged.

"Perhaps he resents car salesmen advertising on his vehicle. Every time I buy a car, the first thing I do is to rip the dealership's advertising sticker off the back window. I don't want to give the dealer free publicity."

I took a fresh tissue and rubbed a little harder, this time going right to the edge of the plate.

Bra – We – Ca –

"West Bradford Wedding Cars," Max read aloud.

I stood up, putting a hand to my aching back.

"That doesn't sound like a car dealership to me."

"Allow me to capture the evidence."

After passing me the box of fairy lights to hold for him, Max pulled from a trouser pocket a small silver device the size of a matchbox. I wondered how he ever found anything with so many trouser pockets to choose from.

When he put the device to his eye, holding each end delicately between thumb and forefinger, I realised it was a tiny camera. Max always welcomed an excuse for a bit of light espionage. He squatted to click a close-up shot of the registration plate.

"Now that I do find intriguing. Earl told me when he arrived in school that the car belonged to him. Does this mean he's got an *alter ego* running a wedding car hire business up north?"

"Maybe he preferred it to the standard airport hire car," I suggested. "He likes status symbols."

"Surely he wouldn't have flown into Bradford? Does Bradford even have any incoming transatlantic flights?"

He pulled out his phone for a quick search online.

"Leeds Bradford Airport currently has precisely one flight from the US, and that's from New York. Otherwise it serves only Europe. Surely if Earl was coming from the Deep South, as he claims, he'd have flown into Heathrow or Gatwick and used one of their airport car hire firms? Surely they'd have top of the range models available."

"We only have his word that he came straight here from the airport," I observed. "He might have diverted north for other business first."

Max strode round to the back of the car, and I stooped to wipe the graffiti and the white paint off the rear licence plate too. Max photographed that plate, then stood back to take pictures of the car from all angles.

"If he's purposely painted out the company name, there's a reason for it," he said when he'd finished. "We'd better cover it up again before he notices we've rumbled his little secret. I'll nip round to maintenance now and nab a drop of whitewash to do the honours. You get back into school and leave this to me. Once I've got the firework lights set up, I'll do a little research. I feel some Googling coming on."

Glad to abdicate that responsibility, I went back indoors to prompt the girls to change into warm clothes ready for the bonfire party. I wondered whether Earl would join the festivities. As an American, would he even know what Guy Fawkes Night was?

10

Sparks Fly

Not long after all the girls had assembled on the playing field for the bonfire night party, Joe had appeared at my side, looking unusually rugged for term-time in a waxed jacket, jeans and wellies.

"I think Max misses playing with dynamite," I smiled.

Like Joe, Max preferred to keep his past shrouded in secrecy. Perhaps that common ground was one reason they'd become firm friends. I was forever trying to winkle out of Joe exactly what Max had done in his former career, but he only ever gave me vague clues. Although disappointed, I was glad Joe was such a loyal friend.

"I think so too. Although he's more used to defusing than igniting explosives."

"It must have taken him a while to overcome his trained instincts and light fireworks instead of extinguishing them."

Joe was standing so close that it would have felt natural to slip my gloved hand into his, had we not been in the company of a hundred keenly observant girls.

"Old Hairnet's thankful that's the case. She doesn't have to worry about health and safety tonight, knowing Max is in charge."

Max had organised the show with the thoroughness of a military campaign. Before any of us arrived, he'd set up the display, nailing Catherine wheels to posts, sticking rockets in bottles sunk into the ground, and planting the bases of Roman candles in compacted piles of damp sand. Fire buckets of water were lined up like troops reporting for duty. Several metres in front of the fireworks, he had unfurled a low white picket fence, posts linked by twisted wire, to stop girls wandering into the danger zone.

To the right of the fireworks, a huge bonfire, ready to light, was surrounded by flame-proof mesh, allowing the crowd close enough to benefit from its warmth without risking burns. Inner warmth would be provided by steaming home-made soup, sausages in bread rolls, parkin and hot chocolate, laid out on trestle tables, courtesy of Miss Button's cookery class. To the left of the food stall, a large wooden garden chair stood empty.

The Bursar stomped over to join me and Joe. In his duffel coat, flat tweed cap and green wellingtons, he looked like Paddington Bear on a country retreat.

"Such a shame Miss Harnett is against burning a guy on the bonfire," said the Bursar, brandishing a box of matches and a packet of long tapers. "I know who I'd like to burn in effigy just now."

He glared across the field to St Bride's House. Illuminated by the night security light, Earl Bunting was strolling across the forecourt to join us.

"Even if she let us, it would feel wrong to burn a guy of Earl," I said with a grimace. "It would feel like we were sacrificing Lord Bunting."

"If we don't look at Earl, he might not notice us," murmured Joe, but to no avail. Earl was striding towards us as if confident of a welcoming reception.

"Hey, Jim, how do you fancy joining me for a swim Saturday?"

He meant Joe, of course. The Bursar slipped away towards the bonfire. Joe coughed.

"No can do, Earl, not in term-time. I'll be tied up with sports matches."

Joe folded his arms. Even in the darkness, I could tell he was frowning. Earl was teasing him, knowing Joe would have to reveal his true identity if he joined him in the pool. He could hardly turn up on the poolside in a bikini. Even Joe didn't push his luck with his disguise by trying to take the girls for swimming lessons. A specialist swimming coach from the local council pool came in once a week for that.

"I don't suppose I can tempt you, Miss Kidd? Seems a shame to see that pool go unused between the girls' lessons. Swimming alone is never much fun."

He looked me up and down as if assessing what I might look like in a swimsuit. I was glad my thick down-filled coat added many centimetres to my girth.

"Sorry, Earl, I can't swim," I lied.

He took a step closer.

"Oh, but I can teach you. I could swim like a fish from boyhood. Learned in the Mississippi when I was knee-high to a cricket."

I attempted to divert him with a joke.

"Quite the Tom Sawyer. This white picket fence should make you feel right at home."

He didn't smile.

"Why don't you ask Oriana?" said Joe. "She adores swimming. Can't keep her out of the pool. Look, there she is, over by the sweet stall."

"Candy stall," I translated for him.

Earl brightened.

"Do I spy toffee apples? My favourite!"

He strode over to queue-jump the girls, who were politely waiting their turn to receive their ration of one each. Miss Button and her star pupil Issy were doing their best to cater for the hordes before the bonfire was lit.

I waited until Earl was out of earshot before speaking.

"I didn't know Oriana was a keen swimmer."

Joe grinned.

"She's not, she hates it as it messes with her hair. But for Earl's benefit, I daresay she's capable of morphing into a mermaid."

The Bursar was circling the bonfire now, prodding it with a broom handle as if goading a sleeping dragon. Imogen and two of her friends, Amelia and Rose, came to join us, mouths gleaming with a thin residue of red toffee.

"He's checking it for hedgehogs, Miss Lamb," said Imogen.

"You always have to check bonfires for hedgehogs before you light them," added Amelia.

"Or any other living creature," said Rose.

Max's health and safety talk at morning assembly must have sunk in.

"You haven't got a toffee apple, Miss Lamb, nor you, Miss Spryke," said Rose. "We'll go and get you one before they run out. There's exactly enough for one each, including grown-ups."

Before I could refuse, they'd run off, giggling and sliding on the wet grass.

Joe sighed.

"It'll take my playing field weeks to recover from this jamboree. Still, the girls enjoy it."

"Don't you?"

He shook his head.

"It may seem ridiculous considering that for years I competed in a potentially dangerous sport, but I've never been comfortable around fireworks, even sparklers. It's literally playing with fire."

"Yes, but with Max and the Bursar in charge –"

The girls returned with our toffee apples before running to join the circle forming around the bonfire. The Bursar had laid down his stick and was lighting a taper.

"But I must admit, I do like a well-managed bonfire," said Joe. "Come on, let's go and enjoy it."

Trying to bite my toffee apple without getting it stuck to my hair, I went with Joe to join the crowd, filling a gap beside Judith Gosling. Unfortunately, Earl Bunting had the same idea.

"Say, Miss Goblin," he elbowed his way in between Judith and me, "as history teacher, you're the best one to fill me in on this quaint English ritual of yours. Who was this guy Mr Fawkes anyway?"

With her eyes on the Bursar as he moved in and out of the shadows, touching his taper to the huge pyramid of scrap wood, Judith recited the potted history she'd explained to the girls that morning.

Earl whistled.

"So, you burn the poor guy? Doesn't sound to me like something a civilised nation should be celebrating."

"Says the native of a part of his country that once tolerated the Ku Klux Klan," retorted Judith.

Earl seemed scarce able to believe someone might criticise him.

"Not me personally, honey. I have no truck with the Klu Klux Klan, no sir."

He turned and marched away, and Judith tutted.

"Now that I do believe, as he can't even get their name right. Rookie error: it's Ku, not Klu. Comes from the Greek for circle, kykloo."

I often wish I'd studied Classics so that I'd know things like that.

I watched to see who Earl would target next. Oriana's turn came at last. She smiled as he came to stand beside her, and immediately engaged him in animated conversation, pointing at the various parts of the bonfire as the Bursar ignited them. At least if Earl was at Oriana's side, he could do no harm to the girls.

Where had Miss Harnett got to all this time? She was only just emerging from the building, bundled up in a huge paisley shawl around the shoulders of her dark woollen overcoat, a navy waterproof cloche hat pulled down over

72

her ears. She bustled around the perimeter of the bonfire, greeting the girls in turn and stopping here and there to answer a question or listen to a joke. Vicariously enjoying her young charges' pleasure, she seemed in her element. Even the older pupils were visibly excited, the darkness allowing them to channel their inner child without fear of looking immature.

For a while, the air was filled with the crackling and snapping of dry branches, saved for weeks by the gardeners and stored under cover to ensure a good burn. Sparks rose up into the air and floated away into the night sky, clear and starry above us. Who needs fireworks when you've got a good bonfire to watch?

I suddenly thought of Miss Harnett's cat, whom I'd last seen basking by the log fire in her study on Monday, and turned to Joe.

"I hope poor McPhee isn't spooked by fireworks."

Having finished his toffee apple, Joe took aim at the bonfire with the stick, setting a bad example to the girls, childishly pleased when he hit his target.

"Don't worry, McPhee will be locked up securely in Hairnet's study with a bowl of treats. She leaves BBC Radio Gloucestershire on for him. It's his favourite station."

Once Miss Harnett had completed the circuit, she made herself comfortable on the large wooden throne that had been standing empty until now. Miss Button immediately despatched Issy to her with a mug of steaming soup. Perhaps Miss Harnett's teeth weren't up to dealing with a toffee apple.

I gazed around the ring of girls, smiling at the rapt looks on their faces. The younger girls were holding hands, nervous of the dark. Even some of the older girls were linking arms or draping them around each other's shoulders. One of the more anxious new girls sidled over to sit on the arm of Miss Harnett's chair. Miss Harnett didn't seem to mind.

It wasn't just the bonfire that was making me glow inside. It was the sense of being part of this community. We were all at one.

But then – crack! A flurry of sparks shot out from the side of the bonfire at shoulder height. A whooshing sound suggested a rocket had been secreted in the woodpile, and it was heading straight for Miss Harnett's chair.

11

Given a Rocket

The reactions of the girl at her side were faster than Miss Harnett's. Quick as the flash of the explosion itself, the child wrapped her arms around her Headmistress and ducked them both down below the rocket's flight path. The firework soared over their crouched figures, the burnt-out stick coming to rest a hundred metres away on the field beyond.

There was a collective gasp before the girls and staff flocked to their Headmistress to make sure she and her young companion were unscathed. The Bursar stared dumbfounded at his glowing taper as if he thought he had unwittingly sabotaged the bonfire himself.

When Max came running over from the firework area, I excepted him to disperse the girls and send them all indoors for safety. Instead, unseen by anyone else, he darted into the shadows, located the fallen stick, inspected it in the circle of light from his head torch, and slipped it into one of the deeper pockets of his combat trousers. By the time he came over to see Miss Harnett, she'd already taken charge of the situation.

"No cause for alarm, girls. Just an extra dry stick catching fire. It happens all the time with a well-prepared bonfire. Now, on with the sparklers!"

Such calm in the face of a crisis was a good life lesson for the girls and for us all.

Miss Harnett looked about her for assistance. "Bursar, let's be having you! Girls, form an orderly queue!"

Even the timid child rallied at this command. Before long the pupils, as well as some staff, were twirling across the field, zigzagging and looping sparklers in the chill night air, writing their names at high speed before their sparkler could burn out – easier for the Amys and Emmas than the Isabellas and Hermiones among them.

"Soup time!" cried Miss Button as the last sparkler fizzled out.

As soon as each girl had collected a mug of soup, they gathered around the firework fence, where Max stood poised to light the first Roman candle. Then it was the staff's turn to be served. Miss Button slipped out of her pocket a slim, dark bottle and a stack of tot-sized paper cups.

"Sloe gin, ladies," she beamed, handing us each a cupful. "Made by me, not by the girls, last winter."

Gratefully we sipped our ration of the invigorating liquor. Only Miss Harnett, whose smile seemed a little fixed, received a second helping of this precious nectar.

The Bursar bustled up to join us.

"My dear Headmistress, I cannot imagine how that rocket got into the woodpile. It was a rocket, you know. Max found the stick, complete with remnants of the paper casing and explosive. I assure you I did all the necessary safety checks, but I had no idea. I could not possibly legislate for concealed explosives. Only for hedgehogs."

He turned to the rest of us.

"Do any of you know of a disgruntled girl who might have played such a prank?"

We all looked at each other, shaking our heads. The idea of any of the girls attacking their beloved Headmistress was preposterous. They were as likely to assault their own grandmothers.

Then Earl appeared, clapping one hand on my shoulder, the other on Judith's.

"Come on, guys! You're missing all the firework action."

He tried to steer us around to accompany him to the firework display, but Judith and I both wriggled free of his grip. He shrugged, as if it was our loss, not his, and moved across to invite a grateful Oriana instead.

I looked down into my paper cup, wishing it could magically refill itself. After tossing our empty cups into the recycling box beside the food table, the rest of the staff ambled across in the direction of the chorus of "oohs" and "aahs", all except Miss Button. She turned her back on the display to attend to the barbecue, long tongs glinting beneath the sparks above our heads.

I felt Joe's hand come to rest reassuringly on the small of my back. Glancing behind us to check no-one was looking, I saw the only sign of life beyond the still blazing bonfire: the small black face of McPhee in the staffroom window. Ever the escapologist, he must have found his way out of Miss Harnett's study, picking up on the danger that had befallen his mistress. Silently he awaited her safe return.

I touched Joe's arm for attention.

"You know Oriana far better than I do. Do you really think she's set her sights on marrying Earl?"

When he laid his hand on my shoulder, I shrugged it off, thinking it hypocritical to throw myself at Joe while berating Oriana's overzealous bid for Earl.

"Unless a better offer turns up. Any newly widowed fathers looking likely since half term?"

"No. I thought she was going to play it cool for a while to recover from the unfortunate incidents of the first half of term."

He gave a wry smile.

"I'm afraid she's of the view that the best thing to do after falling off a bicycle is to jump back on."

I grinned up at him in the dark.

"Well, you should know all about that."

He laughed.

"Yes, but at least I'm more discerning in my choice of bicycles."

Suppressing an indignant guffaw, I elbowed him in the ribs in reproach. Then I noticed Oriana and Earl standing together in the crowd.

"Do you know, I'm half expecting Oriana to come down to breakfast tomorrow in a crinoline and ringlets, channelling her inner Scarlett O'Hara for Rhett Butler over there. She could make a stunning entrance, flouncing down the marble stairs."

Joe harrumphed.

"Frankly, my dear, I don't give a damn."

He edged a little closer, our bodies now touching from hip to shoulder all down one side.

"But I tell you what, if it wasn't for my disguise, and the hordes of girls in front of us, and the beady eye of the staffroom, I'd be more than happy to demonstrate Rhett and Scarlett's famous first kiss just now." He peered through the darkness to gauge my reaction. "But only if that's OK with you, of course."

I'd never had a courtship quite like this before.

"Well, la-di-da," I said, mixing up my movies in my excitement. "Tomorrow is another day."

12

Another Day

Even for Oriana with her proven wardrobe skills, an overnight transformation into Scarlett O'Hara might have been a challenge too far. Instead when she came into the staffroom next morning, she was the image of Jackie Kennedy. Her backcombed blow-dried hairsprayed bob was as sleek as the plain A-line dress beneath it, adorned only by a loose white belt just above the hips. Pearl earrings and matching necklace added a whiff of affluence, as did her low, broad-toed patent leather court shoes. How on earth does she find space to house so many outfits in her compact staff flat? Her wardrobe must be of Narnian proportions.

At her side in his usual camouflage combat gear, Max looked like her personal security detail, despatched by the White House to keep admirers at bay. Max was seldom seen in the staffroom, so I guessed he had come on a mission relating to the previous night's events.

Interrupting the teaching staff milling around Old Faithful, caffeinating up for the morning's lessons, he stood with his back to the closed door, put two fingers in his mouth and whistled for our attention. The low hubbub of pleasantries ceased as we all turned to listen.

"OK, troops, intel needed. Last night, did any of you see any of the girls tampering with the bonfire before it was lit?"

There was a communal murmur of denial.

"Or anyone else? Any adults?"

Slowly he panned the room, making eye contact with each of us in turn. Even though I was innocent, I felt the colour rise to my cheeks.

The Bursar raised his hand.

"The only person I saw in front of the school after dark was Miss Lamb, and she was nowhere near the bonfire. If she was sabotaging anything, it was Earl Bunting's car."

I folded my arms.

"Oh thanks, Bursar! If you were paying attention, you'd have seen that I was committing the opposite of sabotage, checking the girls had cleaned every scrap of mud off Earl's car. Max can testify to that, can't you, Max?"

Max raised his hand.

"Copy that, Gemma. But after you'd left, Earl came to check up on his car. So, he was out there too."

Joe frowned.

"Did you see him go back inside the building after he'd looked at his car?"

"No. He was still there when I went to fetch the sand buckets. So, if anyone had a chance to plant a rogue rocket in the bonfire –"

Max passed a hand across his face in thought.

I wasn't convinced.

"But how would Earl know where to aim it? That is, if you think he was targeting Hairnet."

Mavis raised her hand.

"Her chair was already out there in its usual spot for fireworks night."

"But he's never been to a St Bride's Guy Fawkes party before. How would he know she'd sit there? I didn't, until she sat in it."

Mavis shrugged.

"A reasonable guess? Or he could have been tipped off by any of the girls or staff who are not in their first year here."

Oriana threw up her hands.

"Oh, for goodness's sake, Max, aren't you overdramatising here? Why on earth would Earl, or anyone else, try to shoot a rocket at Hairnet? What could anyone gain by it? It's hardly a murder weapon."

"Depends where it strikes you," replied the Bursar. "Suppose Miss Harnett hadn't ducked, and it had caught her in the face?" He flinched. "Or that little girl sitting beside her?"

We all stared at Oriana. Was she being deliberately obtuse, or just trying to protect Earl?

Max broke the silence to answer Oriana's question.

"To intimidate her?"

Cue sharp intake of breath around the room.

Judith Gosling, ever sensible, put up her hand. "But why? He's already convinced her of his right to the estate. What more could he want?"

Oriana ran her fingers through her perfectly coiffed hair, inadvertently leaving a strand sticking upright, defying gravity beneath its thick hairspray.

"That's for me to find out," said Max quietly. Reaching one hand behind his back, he pulled open the staffroom door. A second later, he was on the other side of it, closing it behind him.

* * *

Fortunately, the girls seemed to have forgotten the alleged rocket attack. Miss Harnett's calm at the moment of crisis had extinguished any fear of danger. Over Friday lunch, they were far too distracted by the other events of the evening – the sparklers, the fireworks and the seasonal banquet – to include the stray rocket in their conversation.

"Of course, it was the Chinese who invented fireworks," said Imogen, taking a croissant from the basket offered by her neighbour. She took the basket and offered it back.

"Chimpanzees?" cried a girl who I'd told off only that morning for not listening properly in class.

The rest of the girls fell about laughing, spreading crumbs across the gleaming tabletop.

"The Chinese, silly," replied Imogen. "The Chinese invented all sorts of cool stuff. Like balloons and –"

She paused. I came to her aid.

"And paper. And printing, both woodblock printing and movable type. A hugely civilising influence on the world."

"And then gunpowder to blow it all up again," said Grace cheerfully. "Does that count as recycling?"

"They weren't much good at cutlery, though, were they?" Imogen held up her fork, touching the prongs with the tip of her finger. "I mean, any fool could stick a few chopsticks together to make a fork. But did they? No."

"Don't be so racist," said Grace, prodding Imogen's arm with her own fork.

"Would Guy Fawkes have had fireworks at the first ever Guy Fawkes night or did they come later?" asked the author of the chimpanzee theory. "Was he having a fireworks party to celebrate blowing up the Houses of Parliament?"

I sipped my black coffee.

"Not so much as a sparkler," I replied. "That's the point of the story, remember? Guy Fawkes and his co-conspirators were caught before a single spark might fly. That's why the fifth of November became a cause for celebration – because the Gunpowder Plot failed. We celebrate the survival of our seat of government. Guy Fawkes isn't the hero, he's the villain."

Democracy seemed the least of the girls' interests.

"If I have a boy when I grow up, I think I'll call him Guy," said Imogen. "It's a nice name."

"You can't do that," said Grace. "It would be like calling your daughter Girl."

Imogen was not deterred.

"And I could call my daughter Sparkler. Or Sparky for short."

"It would be cool if she was born on the fifth of November," said Lily. "My dad's girlfriend is called Holly because she was born on Christmas Day."

Imogen frowned.

"What a rubbish day to be born. I mean, what bigger competition could you have for your birthday than the Baby Jesus?"

Lily nodded.

"Still, at least you don't have to buy him a present."

Their conversation continued at a lively pace until they had finished eating, but I tuned out until it was time to dismiss them.

By the time lunch was over, I was wondering whether Max had planted the rocket himself to try to incriminate Earl. He'd certainly taken against him – but so had we all, except Oriana.

As I left the dining room and caught sight of Earl lingering under his ancestor's painting, I was struck all over again by how incongruous his presence was in our safe little world of St Bride's. I detoured to talk to him, wondering whether to raise the issue of the company name on his car registration plate, turning over in my mind different ways I might casually bring up the subject.

"Say, Earl, what did you think of West Bradford?" or "So, are you back off to Yorkshire soon?"

At the sound of my footsteps, he turned round, flashing a forced smile. I ventured a harmless opener.

"You must know that portrait like the back of your hand by now."

"I guess I'm still getting used to the life-sized version after my introduction to it online." He smoothed his hair with the palm of his hand to replicate the perfect grooming of his ancestor in the portrait. "First time I saw it, he was just the size of a postage stamp, but I spotted the resemblance straight off. I thought once I enlarged it, differences would appear. But no, the guy just got more real. Gee, standing here now I feel as if I'm looking in a mirror."

Joe strolled up to join us, polishing a hockey stick with a cloth. I wondered whether he was trying to look threatening. A hockey stick would make a good weapon.

"Then it must have given you a turn to see Lord Bunting's effigy in the mausoleum, complete with death mask?"

"Effigy?" Earl's eyes widened. "You mean a scarecrow, like that guy Fawkes the girls were telling me about? You'd burn your benefactor?"

Joe and I exchanged glances.

"No, I mean the sculpture of Lord Bunting in the mausoleum. Surely you saw it on the tour Oriana gave you? You know, the one where he's lying down on his tomb?"

Earl shook his head.

"Why, no, siree. She may have pointed out the building, but she didn't offer to take me inside. Besides, I had no great desire to see myself looking dead."

He gave a laugh as phony as his smile.

That wasn't how Oriana had described that part of the tour. She'd said Earl Bunting had declined her invitation to see his ancestor.

"Really? If I had just discovered I had an ancestor sufficiently important to have his own mausoleum, I'd have visited it to pay my respects and feed my curiosity the first chance I got."

Earl gazed into the distance.

"I guess I'm still having trouble adjusting to my birthright. As I told you before, Miss Lark, where I come from, to be born out of wedlock is still a shameful thing, which is why my momma kept it from me for so long – and why my great-great-great-however-many-times grandmother never let on to a soul the truth about her baby's daddy. When she arrived in the Land of the Free, she told everyone she was a widow. I guess she had an honest face because until that photo popped up on Twitter, she had gotten away with it."

Then his shoulders relaxed, he slipped his hands into the pockets of his flannel trousers and gave a rigid smile.

"Still, I'm not the only one around here with an interesting past, am I, Miss Bike?"

He emphasised the word "Miss".

Joe stared at his hockey stick, picking at an imaginary splinter.

Earl continued unabashed. "And wouldn't we sometimes rather our past stayed in the past?"

With a smug grin in my direction, Earl sauntered off down the corridor, whistling *Dixie*.

13

Time Out

Two weeks later, Oriana was on duty in the entrance hall after breakfast, waiting until the last girl in our House had departed for the exeat weekend. Just as the great front door closed behind the final straggler, I came down the stairs to find her sitting on the sofa, lapping up the peace and quiet.

"Nice day for your excursion," I said, trying to sound pleased that she finally had the privacy for a proper date with Earl. So far he'd taken her for the odd spin in his Rolls-Royce on her evenings off, but always with the proviso that she had to return to her own flat – without him – and her housemistress duties by midnight.

"Will you be away overnight?"

I kept my voice casual, not wishing to sound judgemental.

Her Jackie Kennedy look had left Earl unimpressed, so today she had gone for the preppy look: neat blazer, crisp shirt, chino skirt and penny loafers. She brushed a stray hair from her lapel.

"Why, are you wondering whether you can sneak Joe into your flat in my absence?"

A school rule forbade staff from entering each other's accommodation to ensure we each had a private space for the sake of our sanity. I sat down beside her so I didn't have to look her in the eye.

"No, just wondering whether to look out for you at bedtime. I'm staying in school all weekend. I don't want to lock you out if you're coming back."

She shrugged.

"It's not your worry. Now the Bursar's living in the old butler's flat, he'll take care of that. You're free to do as you please." She gave me a taut little smile. "It's between you and your conscience." She got to her feet. "Now, here's Earl. I'll be off."

Earl, dapper as ever, marched across the hall and gave Oriana a little bow, before reaching for her hand to lead her out to his car as if inviting her to join him for the next polka. As I closed the front door behind them, I wondered how Oriana had turned my gentle enquiry into casting aspersions on my morals.

I'd arranged to meet Joe for a walk around the school grounds to enjoy the last of the autumn colour. One strong gale and the remaining few golden leaves would be gone. Then we were going out to Wendlebury Barrow for a pub lunch. I was glad I had my own car to drive us. The sky was overcast and the wind piercingly loud, so there was no way I'd agree to cycle there, as Joe and I had done before half term.

When Joe caught up with me, I was pleased to see he was wearing holiday civvies, men's jeans and a cream Aran cabled sweater.

"I suppose Earl's family back in the States must have done well for themselves if he can afford to hire such a fancy car while he's here," he commented as we crossed the damp grass towards the lake. "Perhaps he has Lord Bunting's entrepreneurial genes. When you think how well Lord Bunting did for himself while barely leaving his estate, it makes you wonder what dizzy heights he'd have reached if he'd ventured further afield."

As we strolled around the picturesque perimeter of the lake, I decided that had I been Lord Bunting, I would have stayed on my estate too. I bet I wasn't the only member of staff to pretend during school holidays that St Bride's House and its gardens belonged to me.

Joe kicked a pebble into the lake.

"I think that Rolls-Royce is wasted on him, though," I said, hoping to make him feel better. "I heard him apologising to Oriana last night that he didn't have something more luxurious for their date. He says his cars back in the States are all much bigger."

"Cars plural?" Joe sniffed. "And here's me with no car at all."

"It might be all talk, though. We'll find out if and when they arrive."

"He's bringing them to England?"

"So he says. Along with a lot of personal possessions. All coming by sea, apparently, which is why they're taking so long. They're due to arrive after Christmas. That's his story, anyway."

Joe pulled a dry reed out of the bank and started splitting it lengthways with a fingernail.

"It doesn't take that long to ship stuff from the States. Are you sure?"

I nodded.

"So Oriana told me. She reckons it's a sign of his intention to stay here for good. I don't think she'd be so set on him if this was just a flying visit. She's no desire to go live in the States. Her roots are here at St Bride's, same as Hairnet's."

I paused to pick up a leaf skeleton from the grass and held it up to the light. The silver-grey sky shone coldly through the rusty lace.

"We've got to stop her, Gemma."

If I hadn't known that Joe and Oriana's relationship was like brother and sister, I might have been jealous. But he just wanted to protect her feelings, ever at risk thanks to the frequency with which she threw herself into inappropriate relationships.

We reached the bench where, on the previous exeat, we'd sat to feed bread to the ducks. A couple of mallards hauled themselves out of the water to waddle about at our feet, hoping for scraps. I pulled from my coat pocket half a croissant that one of the girls had left on her plate at breakfast, passed half to Joe and started to flake my share. When I threw the first few crumbs on the grass, the ducks quacked their appreciation.

"It does seem a bit fast to make such a huge commitment," I remarked. "I could understand him coming over to establish his ownership of the estate and then going back to live in the States. But to move lock, stock and barrel into the midst of a busy, purposeful community is quite a step. It's not as if the house were empty."

Joe touched my hand.

"Commitment, eh? That old chestnut."

"It's not just a question of moving house. It's moving countries."

"And cultures," put in Joe. "There's a bigger gulf between the US and the UK than the Atlantic. To be fair to Earl, I think he is trying. Mavis told me she'd spotted him reading *Debrett's* in the school library the other day. I heard him say before the bonfire party that he welcomed the opportunity to embrace a British tradition. Guy Fawkes Night must seem bizarre to those who've not grown up with the concept."

A third duck sped across the lake to join his comrades' impromptu picnic. Rather late to the party, a peacock wandered down from the lawn, his tail feathers threadbare from his autumn moult. The girls' dormitories were competing to see which could collect the most discarded peacock feathers, despite Mavis Brook's warning that it was bad luck to bring them indoors.

"Unlucky for the peacock, perhaps," was the extent of Oriana's sympathy. It was only a matter of time before a feather appeared as an accessory to one of her outfits.

"Is it, though? Is England so strange to him as he'd have us believe?"

I tore the remaining pastry into pieces, wondering just how small a crumb could be before it cost a duck more calories to peck it up than it gained from eating it.

"What makes you say that, Gemma?"

Croissant gone, I clasped my hands in my lap. Gently, Joe laid a hand over them. It was warmer than any ungloved hand deserved to be in this dank, damp lakeside air. I let it rest there, feeling fortified against the chill breeze.

"Maybe I'm hypersensitive as an English teacher, but it seems to me that he uses more Anglicisms than I'd expect from an American who claims never to have been here. At the bonfire party, I was translating for him – candy stall for sweet stall, for example. Then unprompted, he started talking about toffee apples. Don't they call them candy or taffy apples over there?"

Joe turned to look me in the eye.

"I'm glad you said that, Gemma, as there was something about his conversation that niggled me too. He referred to the Klu Klux Klan. But as Judith pointed out, it should be Ku, not Klu. When I was studying American civil rights for History A Level, our teacher made a big deal out of getting the name right, as it's such a common error among non-Americans at least."

"For someone born and bred in the Deep South, it strikes me as an inexcusable error."

The ducks turned their backs on us and waddled down to the lakeside, splashing as they launched themselves on to the opaque grey water.

Joe interlaced his fingers with mine.

"My goodness, Miss Lamb, we're being frightfully serious for an exeat. Let's go off site and have fun instead."

When he stood up, I reached my hands out for him to pull me to my feet and kept hold of one of them as we continued our walk. We lingered to watch the ducks swim to the far end of the lake, where large fronds of weeping willow were dipping into the surface water, creating a pretty ripple effect. The ducks barged through, the fronds reminding me of the long strips of plastic people hang in their back doors to keep out flies. They hopped on to dry land in front of the grotto, a small rocky cave built in keeping with some romantic Gothic garden trend.

"Those ducks have made me hungry," Joe said. "Let's make it an early lunch."

14

Identity Parade

When we set off, my car was the only one left on the forecourt. As we drove to Wendlebury Barrow, our previous journey by bicycle played on a loop in my mind. My outing with Joe in the earlier half of term had been my first trip on a bicycle for many years. I wondered what other firsts might arise in our relationship this weekend. Could I even call it a relationship yet?

I sneaked a sideways glance at Joe. Of course it was a relationship. Even platonic friendships count as relationships. On that basis, I could even claim a relationship with McPhee.

In our eagerness, we arrived at The Bluebird before it had opened for lunch. Joe nodded up the High Street.

"We've got time for a quick trip to the bookshop, if you fancy it."

I didn't need to be asked twice.

Behind the trade counter, proprietor Hector Munro was typing at his laptop like a demon. Sophie, the girl who runs the tearoom, called out a friendly greeting, welcoming us by name.

"Are you late for morning coffee or early for afternoon tea?" she grinned, wiping an already spotless tearoom table for us.

I was ready for a hot drink of any kind after our chilly lakeside stroll.

"Actually, we've come for a pub lunch, but The Bluebird's not open yet," I explained.

Hector looked up at last. "No, Donald won't open up for another half an hour, folks. Feel free to kill time by buying a book."

We ordered two cappuccinos and sat watching the bookshop's customers browsing the shelves. It was only three weeks since half term, but I'd forgotten how good it felt to be responsible for no-one and nothing but myself. Term-time life at a boarding school is pretty full on. Even in free periods, you're never really off duty.

"So, what's new at St Bride's?" asked Sophie, setting down our drinks. The cups she'd chosen were branded *The Prime of Miss Jean Brodie* for me and *The Odyssey* for Joe. I'd decided to buy some of the shop's book-themed mugs for my parents for Christmas but couldn't decide which titles to choose.

Hector, meanwhile, had set up a song on the shop's hi-fi – Freddie Mercury singing about wanting to ride his bicycle. It's a bit of a game he plays, matching the background music to the customer.

"How are Kate's peacocks getting on?" he asked.

Hector's godmother, Kate, had recently delivered to the school a pair of peacocks which were surplus to village requirements.

I grimaced. "They take a bit of getting used to. They make an awful noise!"

Sophie shuddered.

"Tell me about it. I had one of them camped out in my garden for a few days."

"Almost as bad as pheasants," said Hector. "Although peacocks are slightly less stupid."

Local keepers raise pheasants for shooting, and just then you couldn't drive down certain lanes without almost running one over.

"Do I gather the peacocks are not your only newcomers?" asked Hector. "We had a tall fellow in here the other day, looking for a book about inheritance law. When I asked him for his address to go on our mailing list, he put it down as St Bride's School. But when I asked which subject he taught, he looked blank. I was puzzled as to what his role was, as I know Miss Harnett doesn't recruit any male staff."

"Present company excepted," added Sophie. She and Hector seemed to be in on Joe's secret, as did Donald in the pub. Sometimes I wonder whether it is much of a secret at all.

"You mean Earl Bunting?" I purposely said no more to see what they'd made of him.

"Really? Is he an Earl? I only asked for his surname and initial. I thought it was a coincidence that he was a Bunting. Is he related to the original family?"

Sophie came to join us with a coffee for herself in her favourite *Travels with My Aunt* cup. "He didn't sound like an earl to me, nor did he speak like one. He just sounded like an ordinary Englishman, with no particular regional accent. Not posh, anyway."

Hector laughed.

"People with titles don't all talk like the Queen, Sophie."

Joe and I looked at each other.

"Are we talking about the same person?" said Joe. "The Earl Bunting we're talking about has an American accent. He isn't actually an earl. Earl is just his given first name."

Sitting at the next table, an elderly man in a scruffy tweed jacket and hand-knitted scarf leaned over towards me, jogging his coffee cup so that it overflowed into his saucer.

"Are you talking about that poncey moustachioed fellow with the shiny shoes who was up the pub the other day? He said his name was Bunting. I remembered his name because I reckoned he must have got called Bye, Baby at school. Would have done in our playground when I were a lad, anyway. Loud-mouthed American, is that your man? Though to be fair, he got a good round in."

I pulled my phone out of my handbag and summoned up the heritage page on the St Bride's website.

"Let's settle this once and for all." I clicked on the image of Lord Bunting's portrait and enlarged it to full screen size. "Imagine this chap in modern dress."

I handed my phone to the old man, who looked at it before passing it to Sophie.

"Yes, that's him," she said, taking it over to Hector at the counter.

Hector nodded in recognition.

"Handsome fellow," added Sophie. "Was it taken by one of those photographers who gives you historic costumes to dress up in? I've always wanted to go to one of those. Oh no, hang on, it's an oil painting, isn't it? That must have cost him."

Hector laughed.

"It's the portrait that hangs in the school hall, isn't it, Gemma?" he asked. "It's of the founder of the school. But there's a distinct family resemblance to the Mr Bunting who was in here the other day. That's funny, I thought the family line had died out, and the title, with the chap in the painting."

"So did we all," said Joe. "But our visitor claims to be the rightful heir to the estate."

Hector frowned.

"If there wasn't such a striking resemblance, I'd be tempted to cry cuckoo."

"Don't you mean wolf?" asked Sophie.

I reached for Joe's hand.

"Very possibly that too."

15

In The Bluebird

As we crossed the High Street to reach the pub, I slipped my hand through the crook of Joe's arm.

"So why is he changing accents every five minutes? English in the bookshop, American in the pub."

"Because he doesn't understand that people who live in the countryside talk to each other? Unlike in London, where you can live next door to the same person for years without ever sharing a conversation."

"There's also the possibility that he's just plain arrogant and considers himself too smart for us. Classic aristocrat."

Joe mimed a slapped wrist.

"Don't let Hairnet in on your socialist views, Gemma. Remember, we've titles aplenty on the school roll."

I gazed at the cover of the paperback that Hector had just sold me as weekend reading: *Ten Days That Shook the World* by John Reed, an account of the Russian revolution.

I didn't know I needed it until Hector introduced me to it – the sure sign of a good bookshop.

Joe held the pub door open for me and we went inside.

"More importantly, which is his real accent, American or British?"

"Or something else entirely? But hang on, Joe, I've just realised – there's something I haven't told you yet. You know about how the girls muddied his car and I made them clean it off again?"

He chuckled at the memory.

"Yes."

"Well, I made a discovery. On the registration plate, beneath a layer of white paint, is the name of a car hire firm."

"No shame in hiring a car. Except that he's already told us he owns it."

"Yes, he's told Oriana the same," I said, thinking of her out on her date with Earl in that very car.

Joe led the way to a table for two beside a pleasantly warm radiator.

"No? So why would he cover up the name of the car hire firm, unless he didn't want us to know where he got it from?"

Donald came out from behind the bar to bring us a couple of menus.

"Good afternoon, you two. Lunch, is it? Can I get you any drinks while you look at the menu?"

"Lime juice and soda for me, please, Donald," I said. "I'm driving."

"Half a cider for me, thanks."

Donald left the menus on the table.

"So, don't keep me in suspense, Sophie. Where did he hire it from?"

"It looks like he hired it from West Bradford Wedding Cars."

"West Bradford Wedding Cars?" Joe echoed. "Are you sure? Hardly the obvious place for him to hire a car. Unless he's planning to grant Oriana's wish sooner than even she might hope."

"I doubt it. Which makes me wonder whether he's either the firm's proprietor or a car thief."

"Wow." Joe picked up a menu. "I suggest we order our lunch before we go any further. Let's have something we'd never have at school. The pies here are legendary."

"So's the Loch Ness Monster, but I wouldn't want to eat it."

But I needn't have worried. The fluffy puff pastry gleamed golden beneath its baked-on egg glaze, concealing a glistening filling of chunky beef darkened by stout-enriched gravy. For a while our food distracted us from our pursuit of Earl.

Eventually I set my knife and fork down across my empty plate.

"If Earl secretly owns a car hire company, maybe he's got his eye on St Bride's as a posh wedding venue," I said. "To be fair, it would make a very good one. But that doesn't explain why he would use two different accents in places practically on top of each other – the bookshop and the pub."

Donald came to remove our plates.

"That was delicious, Donald, thank you."

Joe wiped his mouth with a paper serviette.

"Remember what Earl bought in the bookshop? A book about inheritance law. If he is a real Bunting, he may still be researching the strength of his legal claim. It sounds as if it took him by surprise when Hector asked him for his postal address. I note he was careful not to reveal his full name to Hector or Sophie. Not the Earl bit, anyway, just his initial. But why would he bother trying to keep a low profile in the bookshop when it seems he's been making his mark across the road here, buying Billy and his friends a pint? There's bound to be some crossover in their clientele. There's Billy for a start, and Hector and Sophie often drink in here."

"Who's Billy?"

"That old boy in the tearoom just now. He's a regular."

Donald returned with the dessert menu. I looked at Joe, my hand on my tummy, and shook my head. The weight I'd gained since starting work at St Bride's was no bad thing. Under the pressures of my relationship with my ex, for a long time I'd eaten next to nothing. Even so, there was only so much food I could handle this early in the day.

"Not for us, thanks, Donald," said Joe. "But coffee, maybe, Gemma?"

"Cappuccino, please."

"Make that two, please. Oh, and Donald? Do you remember an American visitor coming in here recently? Tall guy, dapper, dark-haired with a moustache? Stood Billy and his cronies a round of drinks or two."

Donald's response was guarded.

"Is he a friend of yours?"

Joe and I exchanged glances.

"Let's call him a colleague," said Joe. "No, an acquaintance."

Donald picked up our empty glasses.

"No love lost there, I take it?"

I touched my foot against Joe's to caution him against saying too much.

"You could put it that way," said Joe.

"Although we don't really know him well enough to make a proper judgement," I added.

Donald sighed, hugging the glasses to his chest.

"We're getting to know him better than we'd like to here. And seeing him more often than I'd wish."

Joe emptied his glass.

"It's not like you to discourage custom, Donald."

Donald shrugged. "If he was paying his way, I'd welcome him every night. But it's all got a bit awkward."

He gazed down at the glasses in his hands.

"In what way awkward, Donald?" I said gently. "If you tell us, we might be able to help."

"You think so?"

Joe pulled a chair over from the next table and beckoned to Donald to sit down. Donald glanced back at the bar to check whether anyone was waiting to be served. When he saw a pleasant woman of around his own age, presumably his wife, was serving the only waiting customer, he set our empty glasses back down and seated himself. He pulled the chair forward and leaned his elbows on the table, ready to confide in us.

"Well, he first came in just after Bonfire Night. When I went to the car park to put out a crate of empties, I saw a fancy white Rolls-Royce pulling in, and who should get out but your mate."

I flinched at the term.

"Then he goes round to open the front passenger door and out steps that teacher woman whose hair is a different colour every time I see her. You know, the one with the unusual name. I can never remember it. Oceania, is it? Australasia? Not that she comes in very often."

The subtleties of Oriana's sartorial repertoire were clearly lost on Donald. The archetypal pub landlord, he wore the same style all year round – soft cords, checked shirt, and comfy shoes.

"Well, when I saw that Roller, I thought, 'This is a bit of all right'. A fancy car on the forecourt always brings in extra punters. Locals who haven't been through our doors for weeks suddenly swing by celebrity-spotting. Tourists who might otherwise drive straight past call in, assuming it to be a classier joint than it is."

I gazed around the room, taking in the cosy, classic English village pub setting, jam jars of chrysanthemums on every table, log fire blazing, horse brasses gleaming in the firelight. Donald had no need to feel apologetic.

"When they came in, it was obvious the pair of them were trying to impress each other." He broke off and turned to me. "Sorry, Gemma, is that teacher a friend of yours? I don't mean to be rude about her."

"Don't worry, Donald, you're not being rude. Oriana is my friend, but you're just telling it how it is."

"OK, if you're sure. Anyway, he ordered a bottle of champagne, even though he was driving. I thought twice before serving it, as I didn't think his lady friend could drink it all by herself. There's not much of her to soak up alcohol, and I didn't want her to get sloshed or him to exceed the drink-drive limit. But we don't often sell champagne here, and, well, at thirty odd quid a time –"

Joe let him off the hook. "No-one can blame you for taking Earl's money, Donald. You've got a business to run."

Donald's tense shoulders dropped slightly.

"Thanks, Joe. It's not easy keeping a country pub in profit these days, and we have to take whatever business comes our way. Anyway, he was talking quite loudly in this American accent, which made him conspicuous, because we don't often get Americans in during November. So, what with that and the flash car, he was attracting more than his fair share of attention. In no time at all, Billy had sidled up with his unfailing nose for a free drink, brandishing his empty pint tankard. When Earl asked me for a few extra champagne flutes, his bird looked none too pleased. Before long, the whole darts team ended up sitting round their table, enjoying her fella's champagne. He didn't seem to mind, though. He likes to be the centre of attention, that one."

I bit my lip, imagining poor Oriana's frame of mind at that point. I tried to look on the bright side.

"Oh well, he got his money's worth out of his bottle of fizz if it made him Mr Popular for the night."

"You say that, Gemma, but it wasn't his money's worth he was getting. You see, he put it on a tab. I thought, well, no harm in that. It's a dependable sign that a punter's planning to make a night of it and spend a substantial amount. A couple more bottles of champagne followed.

He cleaned my cellar right out, in fact. I don't usually stock many bottles as there's not a lot of demand for it round here. Then he and his lady friend had a lavish steak dinner. He compared it very favourably to a Texas steak, so I was expecting a decent tip at the end of the night. But then at chucking out time, he stands up, pats down his jacket and trouser pockets, and announces he's left his wallet back at St Bride's."

Joe scowled. "Poor Oriana, she'll have found that very embarrassing. I suppose he made her pick up the tab."

At least that was one humiliation Steven had never subjected me to. He always liked to flash his cash.

Donald held Joe's gaze.

"She offered, but he immediately insisted that she put her purse away. Then he told me not to worry, he'd pay next time, and that there'd be no problem. What could I do? All the regulars seemed to like him, and I didn't want to upset any of them, nor put him off returning if he was going to rack up a big bill like that every time."

With a glance at his watch, Donald pushed back his chair and got to his feet, collecting our empty glasses with one hand and our dessert menus with the other.

"So, has he been back since?" asked Joe. "Or is that the last you saw of him?"

Donald tucked the menus under his arm and pulled a bar towel from his belt to wipe the table where our glasses had left wet rings.

"Oh yes, he's been back all right, four times. But he still hasn't paid a penny. His tab's nearing four figures now."

I gasped.

110

"But that's terrible!"

"His parting shot was, 'You know where I live', and that teacher said, 'Not just live there, Earl, you own it now too.' That cheered me up, though it also puzzled me. What's that about? I thought it belonged to your Headmistress."

I chose my words carefully.

"He's definitely a man of means, Donald."

"So you think I'll get my money sooner or later? Thanks, Gemma, that makes me feel better. Now, let me get you those coffees."

I let it go at that, hoping he was right.

"The rotten toad!" said Joe, once Donald was out of earshot. "And poor show from Oriana for not reining him in. If I were Donald, next time he's in, I'd clamp his car."

I grinned. "I bet Mavis would be happy to help you. Do you think we should tell Oriana to gee him up to settle his debt?"

"Trouble is, Oriana's in the same boat as Donald. She wants to keep on the right side of Earl for reasons of her own."

Donald's wife brought over our cappuccinos, sprinkled with cocoa in the shape of a heart, a home-made shortbread biscuit on each saucer. I picked up my spoon to stir in the foam around the edges, trying not to disturb the central pattern.

"And now we've another enigma to solve. Which of Earl's accents is the real thing? If we knew that, we might have more insight into the true nature of his claim to St Bride's."

Joe took a sip of his coffee.

"His American gentleman act does sound over the top, but then I always have thought that style of manners a bit phony."

"Even in Rhett Butler?"

"Oh no, he can get away with it. I mean, he's Clark Gable. Who's to say that both Earl's accents aren't fake, and he's some kind of Walter Mitty, with a dozen different accents and identities doing battle inside his head?"

I dipped my biscuit into my coffee and took a tiny bite to make it last.

"At least that's one thing we can say for Oriana. Regardless of what she looks like on the outside, you know what you're getting on the inside. Deep down, she's genuine and loyal."

"Though often daft," said Joe, not unkindly. "Honestly, for someone so shrewd in so many ways, she makes some dreadful decisions when it comes to men."

"Apart from with you." It was Oriana who had landed Joe his job and anonymity at St Bride's. "If Earl's been making this a regular haunt, we're lucky not to have bumped into them here today."

"Let's hope he's taken her somewhere a bit more special for a change." Joe looked around. "This is a lovely country pub, but not really Oriana's style. Not at the moment, anyway. Maybe if one day she takes up with a gamekeeper…"

I laughed.

"I can't quite imagine her as Lady Chatterley."

I took another sip of Donald's velvety coffee – the perfect choice after our rich steak pies.

"His car wasn't there when we left, so I don't think he's taken her back to Honeysuckle Lodge for a weekend of passion. I don't suppose there's any of that there when the Bursar's in residence."

Joe grinned.

"The presence of eagle-eyed Max across the drive in Rose Lodge might put Earl off his stroke."

That jogged my memory. I set down my empty cup with a clatter.

"Oh, but Max isn't there this weekend. Didn't I tell you? He's taken a run up north, and Rosemary has gone with him, so everyone assumes they're on a mini-break."

"Really? They don't usually take off at exeats. They just batten down the hatches and make the most of some quality domestic time together." Max and Rosemary's marriage was under constant strain in term-time as their shifts didn't coincide, Rosemary working days and Max mostly nights.

"Ah, but this weekend Max is on a special mission. He's gone to check out West Bradford Wedding Cars."

16

In the Swim

As we passed the cottages at the gate on our way back to school, we noticed the white Rolls-Royce parked outside Honeysuckle Lodge. Over the garden wall, flapping in the wind on the washing line, hung a couple of bath towels, a pair of black swimming trunks and a gold bikini.

"Looks like Earl's gone from one extreme to the other with his dating budget," I said. "This morning's date must have been a free trip to the school swimming pool."

We progressed down the long drive, enjoying the view of the main school building, and I pulled into the forecourt to park in my usual space. I was looking forward to our own plans for the afternoon: to watch a DVD of *Gone with the Wind* in my House drawing room. Joe had never seen the film, although he was familiar with its most famous quote. I wanted to refresh my memory of Rhett Butler, wondering whether Earl Bunting was using him as a role model.

Like all the House drawing rooms, ours was full of comfy sofas and armchairs. Having them all to ourselves, we picked the biggest, softest couch. In front of it we positioned the Ottoman full of board games to rest our feet on. With a pot of tea and a tin of biscuits on the coffee table, we were all set to enjoy a cosy private cinema experience, when footsteps in the corridor prompted me to click away from the DVD to television mode.

We'd thought no-one else was in the building, so Joe jumped up to check who the footsteps belonged to.

"Hi, Oriana, hi, Earl," he said loudly, just outside the door.

As Oriana and Earl followed Joe into the room, I muted the television, which was currently showing a documentary about the Sahara Desert.

"Armchair travel, huh?" said Earl.

I smiled at him. "The environmentally-friendly approach to tourism. Cheaper too, which suits my budget. But we were just thinking of watching a film."

Not really listening to my answer, Earl's gaze fell pointedly on Joe, a knowing gleam in his eye. When he made himself comfortable in the nearest armchair, as if he was planning to join us for the film, Oriana's face fell. She couldn't even share a sofa with him. The closest she could get was to perch on the arm of his chair.

Earl was still staring appraisingly at Joe, taking in his masculine clothes, smiling to himself. Joe shifted uncomfortably in his seat. Just as we were bracing ourselves for another veiled threat about revealing Joe's secret identity, Earl appeared to lose interest, turning his attention to the room's décor, surveying it with a critical eye.

"I guess this isn't the original furniture."

He sounded disappointed.

"Goodness, no," said Oriana, slipping an arm along the back of his chair and rearranging her stockinged legs to better visual effect. "The governors sold that off long ago. Besides, the repeated application of multiple girls to any piece of furniture reduces it to shreds within no time at all."

Earl thumped the empty arm of his chair with the air of a car salesman kicking a tyre.

"Still, a shame from my perspective."

I didn't see why his perspective mattered when he wouldn't be allowed in the girls' residential areas for reasons of child protection.

Earl rose to his feet and stretched in an exaggerated manner, as if sitting on such a downmarket chair had already started to cripple him.

"Let's carry on, Oriana." He pronounced the first a in her name to rhyme with "hay". I wondered whether he was doing it on purpose to annoy her. Perhaps he was trying to shake her off, hence all that business with the unpaid bill at The Bluebird.

Undaunted, Oriana beamed, gladdened by the prospect of having him to herself again.

"Yes, we'll leave you to your movie," she said. Movie, not film. I'd noticed several Americanisms like that creeping into her vocabulary lately, as if absorbed by osmosis from Earl.

"It's good to watch a film not chosen to please the girls for a change." I smiled, emphasising the word 'film'. When Earl stared at the empty DVD case on the table, I asked the first thing that came into my head to deflect his attention.

"What are you two up to for the rest of exeat?"

Earl flinched, as if realising for the first time that he was expected to spend the whole weekend with Oriana. She answered for him.

"I'm giving Earl the full tour of the house and grounds today. All the rooms he hasn't been allowed into while the girls are in residence."

That lifted Earl's mood a little. "It's quite the Tardis, this place. There's so much more to it than I'd realised from first impressions."

I wondered whether he'd just given his true nationality away. My heart leapt at a potential clue.

"I didn't know they showed *Dr Who* in the States."

He gawped at me.

"Of course they do. Anyhow, Oriana, we'd better press on."

He ran one hand over his hair, still damp from the swimming pool. Oriana leapt at the opportunity to demonstrate an intimate gesture, reaching up to rearrange a lock of hair that had fallen on the wrong side of his parting. Earl's face went rigid. Did he resent her implied criticism of his grooming, or did he just not like his hair being touched?

Then I realised the cause of his sensitivity. Beneath his dark hair, I could see lighter roots – dark blond, or even ginger. It was hard to tell which, as I was sitting and he was standing. But there was definitely a difference.

Trying hard not to stare, I felt the need to say something conciliatory.

"Did you have a good swim this morning? It's a lovely pool, don't you think?"

I liked it, anyway. A relatively new addition to the estate, it was the gift from a girl's grateful father, its up-to-the-minute architecture the polar opposite of the main school building's.

"Oh, it was OK, I guess." Earl screwed up his face in distaste, which animated the ends of his moustache. "But of course, I'm used to swimming outdoors back home in our glorious southern sunshine."

"In the Mississippi?" I said. "Like Tom Sawyer?"

"Tom Sawyer? Oh yes, the guy with all those Olympic diving medals. Remarkable, huh?"

As soon as they'd left the room, Joe leapt up to close the door to muffle our cries of hilarity. It took us a moment to recover the power of speech.

"Tom Sawyer, the famous Olympic diving medallist," said Joe, clutching his stomach in his mirth.

"No wonder he didn't get my reference about the white picket fence on Bonfire Night! You know the part of the story I mean? Where Tom is told to paint his aunt's white picket fence as a punishment and he persuades all his friends to do it for him."

Joe grinned. "Yes, we read *Tom Sawyer* at school, and I enjoyed it so much I went straight on to *The Adventures of Huckleberry Finn.* As you'd think any child raised in the USA would have done. At least he should have seen the film."

"Or indeed the movie," I added gleefully. "Poor Oriana. Is a personalised Rolls-Royce really worth her putting up with all of his nonsense?"

Joe's smile faded as he returned to our sofa.

"Maybe not the fancy car. But perhaps the lure of joint ownership of the St Bride's estate is."

Sobering, I moved a little closer to him, trying to pluck up the courage to lean into his arm.

"You know, beneath his bluster, I think he's pretty sharp."

"But he just confused Tom Daley with Tom Sawyer."

"Maybe Tom Daley's not as well known in the States, being a British sporting hero. More likely Earl's only interested in his own sporting prowess. Classic narcissist."

I didn't want to say it out loud, but I hoped Earl wouldn't work out that Joe had once been a champion cyclist. I didn't put it past Earl to sell the story of Joe's whereabouts to the papers, especially if he was as short of cash as he appeared to be. Taking on ownership of St Bride's, he'd need a vast amount of money to maintain the place without the school fees that had been at Miss Harnett's disposal. Even though most of the fee income went into paying staff salaries and for food and utilities, the Bursar spent a significant sum on keeping up the fabric of the building and the gardens.

I moved on to a cheerier topic of conversation.

"Let's hope Max comes back from Bradford with enough dirt on Earl to oust him from his ridiculous claim on the St Bride's estate."

I hoped Max's revelations wouldn't come too late.

17

Rent Asunder

The first day back after exeat, we were surprised to learn another staff meeting had been booked for teatime. At the morning's briefing in the staffroom, the Headmistress would not be drawn on the reason for the meeting. She looked tired and drawn although she'd just had a weekend off.

In the meantime, I took the first opportunity I could to extract from Max the outcome of his trip to Bradford. At break, realising I'd left my mobile in my flat, I tucked myself away in the corner of the staffroom window seat and I drew the window curtain around me like a cloak of invisibility before dialling Max's number on the internal phone system.

"Max, it's me, Gemma," I whispered. "How was your weekend?"

I chose my words carefully so as not to give away to eavesdroppers the nature of our conversation.

"Gemma, hi. Good thing I went to Bradford. No wonder we found so little online about West Bradford Wedding Cars. They've shut down. Their premises are deserted. No cars in evidence, although there might be some in the locked garage area behind. Electrified fence all around, a high wall with anti-vandal paint, so I couldn't sneak in for a closer look."

"What about the office?"

"Completely empty. Looks to have been for some time. Broken sign above the shop. Pile of post behind the letterbox, all bills. Ceased trading. Accountancy firm details in the window for creditors to contact. Looks like bankruptcy. Might Earl be the owner, having done a bunk? Next stop, Companies House. How about you? What did he get up to over exeat? Did he stay on site? Did he disappear?"

I lowered my voice further.

"Stayed on site with Oriana."

I hoped anyone hearing might assume I was talking about myself.

Just then, someone whisked the curtain from around me, and I found myself cornered by none other than Earl Bunting. Although he was a good six inches taller than me, the height of the window seat gave me the advantage.

"Bye then, Mum, love you," I said quickly, and put down the receiver. Turning to face him full on, I was determined to make the most of my position of relative power. I flashed an innocent smile. "Sorry, Earl, are you waiting to use the phone?"

Before he could answer, I sidestepped him, grabbed my register, and legged it to the sanctuary of my classroom.

* * *

During the afternoon tea break, we gathered once more in Felicity's classroom for the staff meeting. As I arrived, Felicity was arranging on the windowsill a selection of jam jars filled with gleaming fresh mincemeat, each labelled with a girl's initials.

Swaggering about the room while he waited for everyone to arrive, Earl picked up a jar at random and held it up to the light.

"Say, Miss Button, what have your girls been concocting this morning? Doesn't look like any jelly I've ever seen."

Felicity looked genuinely sorry for him.

"Goodness me, Earl, have you never seen mincemeat before? It's one of the most traditional English Christmas foods you could wish for."

Earl frowned and set the jar down again in a different spot, spoiling Felicity's neat row.

"Doesn't look like any meat I know. Which kind of animal did this used to be?"

Felicity laughed, not unkindly.

"It's not minced meat. There's no meat content at all. In days gone by, mincemeat would have included minced meat, but not these days. We even use vegetable suet in our school recipe to keep the vegetarians happy. It's just all sorts of other sweet and fragrant goodies mixed together: dried fruit, sugar, spices, vegetable suet and a little rum, stirred up and left to mature."

"Fruit? There's fruit in this brown mess?" His thin lips curled in displeasure. "What a waste of good fruit."

"Apples, oranges, lemons, sultanas, currants, raisins. Some people add nuts, but I like to keep allergens out if I can."

"I hope it tastes better than it looks. Do you spread it on toast like jelly?"

Felicity laughed.

"Ooh no, not with raw suet in it. It must be cooked before you eat it. Just you wait and see. We'll be selling mince pies at the school Christmas Fair next month. Then you'll have the chance to discover for yourself just how delicious they are. But first, the mixture must rest for the flavours to develop."

Just then Miss Harnett arrived and went to the front of the classroom. Before making her announcement, she waited until the last few staff members had filed in and sat down, perching on the high stools alongside the cookery workbenches.

Earl went to stand at the front of the classroom as if he were her equal. He towered over her in height, but he had none of her natural authority.

Miss Harnett clapped her hands for silence, as if we were a class of pupils, and we were about as quick to obey. With a fixed smile, she panned the room, making eye contact with every one of us, before pulling from her jacket pocket a set of prompt cards.

I wasn't the only one to be surprised. She usually spoke fluently off the cuff, whether addressing staff, girls in assembly, governors in board meetings or parents on open evenings. Not used to note cards, she immediately dropped them on the floor. When her hands flew to her cheeks in embarrassment, her fingers were trembling.

Earl, in an uncharacteristic show of courtesy, bent to pick them up. As he returned them to her, she avoided his patronising gaze, concentrating on sorting the cards into the correct order before she began to speak.

"Now, my dears." Her voice came out louder than usual, as if she was forcing herself to be brave. "Today I must share an interesting development with you. As you know, I have been fortunate to hold this fine estate in trust for nearly thirty years, responsible in the absence of the true owner for maintaining the school and its property for posterity. It has been –" her voice cracked "– the greatest honour of my life."

She paused and swallowed.

"Now that our new friend here has taken over the mantle of ownership, I find myself relieved of many of the responsibilities that have for so long worn me down."

She forced a smile, as if abdication was her own choice.

"While the Bursar will as ever give the new owner the benefit of his long experience and considerable expertise in managing the estate, Mr Bunting will now take charge of the financial side of things."

Joe, sitting next to me, leaned close to whisper in my ear.

"This is going to be interesting. I wonder whether Earl's found his wallet yet?"

When Miss Harnett fell silent, I feared Joe's comment had put her off her stride. Instead, she was pausing to give way to Earl, who took a step forward and began to address us.

"As Miss Hamlet is well placed to know, maintaining this beautiful historic estate brings financial challenges. I accept that as its rightful owner, this responsibility falls to me." That sounded like good news. "So it will come as no surprise to you all to learn that I must charge the school rent for its continued use of the house and grounds – a cost which until now has been zero, given Miss Hamlet's supposed ownership of the estate. You will also no doubt be pleased to hear, ladies and gentlemen –" he looked pointedly at Joe's lavender tracksuit "– that I have decided to waive the back rent due since the estate passed out of my ancestor's hands. Back rent that should by rights have been paid over the last hundred and twenty years to those in the family tree between the founder and me."

Miss Harnett's fingers curled into tight fists at her sides.

"We have yet to negotiate a reasonable rent, but rent there must be."

I was reluctant to admit this seemed only fair.

The Bursar jumped to his feet.

"Mr Bunting, the school already pays you the only rent we can afford."

Earl narrowed his eyes at the Bursar.

"But you pay me nothing."

"Precisely."

The Bursar sat down abruptly as if he thought he'd sealed the deal. Earl shook his head, like a teacher disappointed at a pupil's failure to correctly decline a Latin verb. Or indeed at one who had just split an infinitive.

"As a fellow businessman, Bursar, you know I must charge you something. I would not insult the school by allowing it to operate rent free. But never fear, I have a reasonable figure in mind, and I have already worked out exactly how you can achieve the rent I am asking. All you need to do is increase each pupil's fee by ten per cent and pass that margin directly to me."

I nudged Joe.

"I told you he was smarter than he seems," I hissed.

The Bursar turned an appealing look on Miss Harnett, but she was gazing at the floor. We all knew that few girls' parents paid the full whack. A couple of pupils with cash-strapped parents had even been admitted free of charge, as Miss Harnett had liked them so much at interview that she couldn't bear to turn them away. The feudal tithe that Earl had in mind would not be as easy a solution as he assumed.

Oriana, sitting at the workbench closest to Earl, stood up and turned to address the rest of us.

"Oh, come on, folks, most of the parents can afford it. Quite a few could pay double without even noticing. Think of young Nadia, who flies in each term from Moscow on her Costa Rican passport with her school fees stashed in her suitcase in used US dollars. To the Nadias of this world, St Bride's school fees are pocket money."

Oriana's comment made me wonder whether she had ever set her sights on Nadia's father.

A ripple of recognition ran through her audience. Miss Harnett looked up, a glimmer of hope in her face.

"I suppose we might increase it for some more than others, provided their parents don't compare notes." Her wide eyes betrayed inner revulsion at such a dishonest tactic.

Earl Bunting smiled, his tongue darting out snake-like between his lips.

"Really, Bursar, it's nothing compared to all the back rent I'm letting you off."

Was that a threat? Was he suggesting he'd call in over a century's theoretical debt if the Bursar denied his tithe?

"There's one other little economy that will help make up the full amount for any parents who don't pitch in their share. I know how much you teachers love living on site. Why, several of you have told me that the beautiful setting at St Bride's spoils you to work anywhere else. None of you would be living in accommodation of this calibre without St Bride's."

Surely he wasn't going to boot us out? Or start charging us rent on our staff flats? That was the whole reason I'd come to St Bride's in the first place, for the free accommodation. Our inclusive board and lodging were also the reason why we accepted a teaching salary below the market rate.

"So, I'm sure none of you will mind making a small sacrifice to ensure you can remain in your precious apartments."

Mavis leapt to her feet in indignation.

"You can't milk us for rent. Our salaries won't run to it. Free board and lodging are in our contracts."

Earl nodded sagely.

"That hasn't escaped my notice, Miss Flood. In lieu of rent, you may teach a few more classes a week for the same pay that you're on now. That will shave at least a couple of whole salaries off the school's wages bill to make up the deficit."

We all looked around to gauge each other's reactions. There were no staff vacancies. Was he talking about redundancies? How else could he cut posts?

As the newest recruit, I felt most vulnerable. On the other hand, my subject was part of the core curriculum, possibly the least dispensable of all. Oriana, as Head of Maths, should also be safe. But Felicity Button's eyes were filling with tears. A girl's education would not be considered incomplete without Essential Life Skills, but it would be much diminished.

The Bursar rose to his feet again.

"Really, Mr Bunting, this is quite the wrong forum in which to discuss such a preposterous and insensitive suggestion. You should have run your thoughts past the Headmistress and me before worrying the staff with mere speculation – something that might never come true."

Earl rubbed his chin as if considering the Bursar's objection.

"But it must. Don't you see? Unless you want me to pursue the issue of back rent due – and possibly a court case for keeping my family's rightful earnings from us for all these years."

The Bursar paled and fell back onto his stool.

"I'm a generous soul, my friends. I'm happy to fall into line with the school timetable. I know you all live by the chiming of the school bell. So, let's begin the new arrangement from the start of the next school year. Bursar, that gives you time to implement the new fee structure. In the meantime, you can pay me a reasonable cash allowance to cover my personal expenses – say, two hundred pounds a week – and I'll settle for swapping my current accommodation with what has until now been the Headmistress's apartment. Oriana tells me they were once the state rooms of Lord Bunting, so I think it's no more than my due to inhabit them as his heir, don't you?"

Miss Harnett's veneer of best behaviour snapped. She let out an animal shriek.

Seeing the girls returning to the courtyard for their next lesson, Earl opened the classroom door and beckoned us all to leave. In stunned silence, we trooped out behind Miss Harnett, who was leaning on the Bursar's arm for support. McPhee, materialising from nowhere, followed at her heels.

18

Cornered

"But how can he? How can they let him?"

Mavis Brook thumped the staffroom coffee table, around which the entire teaching staff had gathered after supper for a council of war.

Nicolette Renoir, Head of French, placed one hand over her heart.

"It is not like Hairnet to give in so easily."

Judith Gosling raised a forefinger.

"I reckon he's got something on her. It must be pretty bad if she's prepared to sacrifice her apartment to keep him quiet."

We all knew how much Miss Harnett adored staterooms, especially sleeping in the original four-poster bed that had once belonged to Lord Bunting. "You mean blackmail?" I flushed as I said the word, avoiding looking at Joe.

Mavis folded her arms across her chest.

"Just let him try and pin something on me. I'd soon teach him a lesson."

"At least it means the Bursar gets his house back," said Felicity. "I thought booting him out of Honeysuckle Lodge was imposition enough."

"Perhaps the Bursar could stay put in the butler's flat and Hairnet could move into Honeysuckle," said Joe. "At least then she'll have a proper house of her own."

I'd thought of this myself after overhearing a conversation between the Bursar and Miss Harnett earlier. Just before lunch, I'd gone to the Bursary to drop off a receipt that had been enclosed with a delivery of books for my department. Before I knocked on the door, I heard voices within.

"You know you will always be welcome to move into Honeysuckle Lodge with me," the Bursar was saying, his voice thick with emotion.

"No, no, Geoffrey," replied Miss Harnett quickly. "The girls need me here, day and night. I need to be within easy reach in case of a crisis."

"But Caroline –"

I'd never heard him use her first name before.

"Will you never give up on me, Bursar?" Her voice cracked.

"Never. You can count on me. Whatever Earl does, I'm on your side."

I couldn't help but wonder what was going on during the long pause that followed. Then came the scraping sound of a chair being pushed back, as if she was about to leave.

As Miss Harnett's footsteps approached the door, I leapt several paces back, pretending I was only just strolling up the corridor towards it.

"Hello, Miss Harnett," I said brightly. "Is the Bursar in his office?"

Her smile was strained.

"Yes. Yes, he is. At least for now."

And with that she turned to go. McPhee, always with her these days, followed close behind.

I decided not to share this private conversation with my colleagues. Miss Harnett and the Bursar were already suffering enough without anyone gossiping about them.

* * *

The next time I saw Miss Harnett was after leaving the staffroom. As I approached the marble stairs, usually out of bounds to pupils, a procession of girls, each carrying items familiar from the Headmistress's study, was following Miss Harnett to the top. She turned in the opposite direction to our House corridor to enter an empty dormitory. It had fallen into disuse a few years before, when the school roll of 150 in its heyday gradually dropped to 100 as single-sex schools started to fall out of favour.

It was Oriana's evening off, so House duties demanded my full attention until I'd completed my lights-out patrol at 9.30pm. When I arrived at the youngest girls' dormitory, expecting to find them all ready for their bedtime story, I was startled to discover their beds empty, although judging by the piles of school uniforms on their bedside chairs, they had already undressed. Surely they hadn't all been kidnapped? Something else was missing, but I couldn't put my finger on it.

Quickly I toured the rest of the dormitories, hoping to find the missing girls visiting friends, but there was no sign of any of them. Nor did the older girls have any clues as to their whereabouts.

"Do you think they've gone to raid the kitchen?" I asked a couple of sixth formers. "Perhaps they planned a midnight feast and needed supplies?"

"I don't think so, miss," said Elisabeth. "They're still working their way through their Halloween tuck. It beats me how they're not all as fat as Sumo wrestlers. Sorry, Yoko." She turned to one of our Japanese pupils, elegant in her silk kimono-style dressing gown.

Yoko covered her mouth with her slender fingertips as she tittered.

"Sumo wrestlers are meant to be fat, silly. That's the point."

Elisabeth returned her attention to me.

"If you want us to help you search, miss, just say. But I shouldn't think they'd be hard to find. Just listen out for them."

Sure enough, as soon as I left our House corridor, I became aware of a high-pitched choral singing of the old lullaby, 'Golden Slumbers', from beyond the top of the stairs. As I hastened down the passage, the song ended, to be followed by the clapping of a single pair of hands. The sound was emanating from the disused dormitory providing refuge for Mis Harnett. Puzzled, I knocked on her door, to be met with her usual sunny "Come in!"

136

The sight that met my eyes almost moved me to tears. Three of the beds had been pushed together, with Miss Harnett, sporting a mauve silk nightie and sage green crocheted bed-jacket, tucked into the middle one. On the beds either side ranged the missing girls in their pyjamas, each with a little offering brought from their own dormitory: a red silk heart-shaped cushion; a multi-coloured coverlet knitted by someone's fond grandma; a teddy bear in a zebra-print onesie. They looked like the Von Trapp family being comforted by Maria during the thunderstorm, only this time it was the children comforting the adult.

On Miss Harnett's lap was an orange plastic pumpkin overflowing with sweets and chocolates, the pooled remnants of the girls' Halloween stashes. On the counterpane lay some of their favourite bedtime story books: *Shocks at the Chalet School* by Elinor M Brent-Dyer, a *Malory Towers* omnibus from Enid Blyton, and a vintage edition of *Anne of Green Gables* by Lucy M Montgomery.

Miss Harnett welcomed me into the throng with an enormous smile.

"Look, my dear, how lucky I am. Such kind girls! My dears, you are a credit to the spirit of St Bride's. But here's Miss Lamb come to round you up for bed – the big lamb shepherding the little lambs, ha ha."

The girls giggled indulgently.

One of the smaller girls, emboldened by Miss Harnett's bad joke, put up her hand.

"Perhaps she should change her name to Miss Sheepdog."

They all fell about laughing again, the lines on Miss Harnett's face softening as she joined in their fun.

"Now, run along, girls, and see if you can tuck yourselves into bed before Miss Lamb catches up with you."

When she wiggled her fingers at them in the manner of running legs, they jumped down and trotted off, chattering. The smallest girl, Abigail, doubled back from the doorway and reached hesitantly towards the teddy in his onesie. She turned wide blue eyes on Miss Harnett.

"You don't mind if I take him back, do you? I think I only meant to bring him for a visit –"

Her eyes filled with tears.

Miss Harnett leaned towards her.

"Do you know, Abigail, I would be very glad if you did. I don't believe Teddy would sleep a wink without you."

Miss Harnett picked up the bear from where he sat beside her and held him up appraisingly.

"What's his name?" she asked the girl.

"Algernon. Although my mum sometimes calls him Ernest."

The Headmistress and I chuckled.

"Well, I shouldn't sleep either if I knew Algernon-Ernest wasn't tucked into bed beside the person who loves him best."

She kissed the top of his furry head before placing the bear into the child's grateful arms.

"Now, off to bed with you both. Good night, Abigail. Good night, Algernon. Good night, Ernest."

She watched Abigail skip off and out of the door before patting the bed to her right, an invitation to sit

138

beside her. McPhee, who had taken cover under the beds during the girls' invasion, crept out from his hiding place, leapt silently on to the bed to Miss Harnett's left and sprawled out at full length.

"I wondered where those girls had got to," I began lightly. But I couldn't hold back my concerns for Miss Harnett for long. "But what about you? Are you comfortable? Do you have everything you need? Can I get you anything?"

I gazed around the long, narrow dormitory, sterile and institutional without the personal clutter of girls and unadorned by the lavish decorative details that characterised Miss Harnett's suite of rooms.

Miss Harnett pressed her lips together as she formulated her reply.

"I am treating this as a learning experience. Sleeping in the same conditions as the girls will enable me to appreciate their needs and to consider improvements to their environment."

She reached out to stroke McPhee, who interpreted her gesture as an invitation to move on to her bed. He moulded himself to the shape her leg made beneath the counterpane and began to purr loudly, his fluffy tummy vibrating.

I didn't know what to say, so I just tried to smile, until a tear trickled down my cheek.

"Take heart, my dear, this too will pass," said Miss Harnett, slipping a hand down to stroke McPhee, who is as comforting as any teddy bear. "But my goodness, I'm tired. The best thing you can do for me is simply to let me sleep. Perhaps the answer will come in my dreams.

Answers often do, you know. Now be a lamb and turn the lights out as you leave."

She put her hand to her mouth as she laughed.

"Oh, I'm sorry, Gemma, I'm getting as bad as the girls. Take my feeble joke as indicative of my exhaustion. But in any case, to me you are indeed a lamb." I was pleased to see the return of the customary twinkle to her eye.

"And you are the best shepherdess. Sweet dreams, Miss Harnett."

"And to you, my dear."

19

None Shall Sleep

When I returned to the younger girls' dormitory to turn out their light, they were still far from asleep, although at least they were now climbing into their beds.

"Miss Lamb, Miss Lamb, we can't possibly let that awful man get away with this," cried Imogen. "What can we do to stop him?"

Grace punched the pillow before she lay down.

"It shouldn't be allowed," she declared. "Just because he's got a famous ancestor."

I was glad to hear this from the granddaughter of a Hollywood film star.

I fetched from the shelf by the door a new book for their bedtime story, one from the delivery I'd received from Hector's House that morning.

"Miss Harnett would be the first to agree with you. But we have to go along with what she says. She knows more than we do about what's going on behind the scenes.

141

There are legal reasons why she has to comply with Mr Bunting's instructions."

I hoped this diplomatic answer would placate them for now.

"So, no more pranks on his car, OK, girls?"

A few of them started whispering excitedly to each other.

"Nor on Mr Bunting himself, nor on any of his possessions." I was picturing buckets of water poised over his study door and a plague of frogs in his bathroom. "Or there'll be no bedtime stories for the rest of term."

"Oh, miss!" The groan went round the room as the girls switched off their bedside lamps in turn, creating a Mexican wave of shadow. When I was the only person left illuminated, sitting in the armchair beneath a pool of light from the old chintz-shaded standard lamp, I opened the book I'd brought to read aloud.

Some might think girls at secondary school are too old to enjoy a bedtime story, and I might have done too before I came to St Bride's. But over the past couple of months, I'd come to appreciate the calming effect of this communal act at the end of each school day, uniting us all beneath the warm blanket of a jolly good book.

I opened *The Adventures of Tom Sawyer* at Chapter One and began to read:

"'Tom!' No answer…"

But as I continued, my mind was still racing with rescue plans for the school, starting with a chat with our resident genealogy expert, Judith Gosling.

* * *

Next day I buttonholed Judith by Old Faithful and asked her to explain Earl's place in the family tree and how he came to be Lord Bunting's heir.

She was less forthcoming than I'd expected.

"It'll take some time to explain all the background," she said, pouring me a coffee before taking her own. "You see, it's not only about what's on the family tree."

I frowned. "But surely the family tree is the ultimate authoritative guide to the genetic line? And if Earl's not on it, he's not a true Bunting."

Judith lowered her voice so much I could scarcely hear it.

"The thing is, Gemma, it's not that simple. There is an illegitimate line of descent. Possibly several of them. Miss Harnett has known for some time. Between you and me, it was always on the cards that a claim like this might arise. That's why she asked me to write the official family tree - to hide the risk. But she swore me to secrecy about it, so as not to worry anyone, so you mustn't breathe a word of it, not even to Joe. So you see, that's why she has been so accommodating to Earl. She knew all along he wasn't necessarily a cuckoo."

My shoulders sagged. Perhaps there was no way out of Earl's coup after all.

Judith patted my hand in reassurance.

"That's also why your predecessor had to leave under a cloud. She effectively invited claims to the estate when she pulled that stupid 'Please retweet' stunt with Lord Bunting's portrait. She included a message saying the school would love to hear from any Bunting family members."

"Earl told me about that. No wonder poor Hairnet was upset enough to sack her."

"But don't despair, Gemma. Just because there are theoretical illegitimate heirs doesn't prove Earl Bunting is one of them. But promise me, not a word of this to anyone else, not even to Joe. Meet me in the library after Sunday lunch and I'll tell you all I know."

For the rest of the week, my imagination went into overdrive.

20

Coppiced

Judith had chosen the best place for our clandestine discussion on Sunday. The library was deserted, because the girls were preoccupied with preparations for the traditional Christmas Fair on the last day of term. All the profits would go to the homeless shelter in Slate Green, the nearest Cotswold market town. Each department would make something to sell on a stall, and there would also be entertainment.

Today and the following Sundays, the drama club would be rehearsing for a traditional nativity play and the choir harmonising Christmas carols to be sung as background music at the fair. Any girls learning musical instruments would be practising in small groups for informal recitals in the tearoom set up for the day in The Trough. Between them, these three activities mopped up all of the pupils. Thus, every girl made a contribution to the event that played to their personal strengths. In Miss

Harnett's eyes, Not Joining In was one of the worst misdemeanours.

This meant that all the teachers, apart from music and drama, had the next three Sunday afternoons free. All the others, apart from Judith and I, were using today as the perfect opportunity to go Christmas shopping.

Judith had spread out across one of the library tables a parchment scroll, on which someone had painstakingly hand-lettered the whole of the Bunting family tree, going back to its origins in the Middle Ages. A gilded and coloured coat of arms adorned the top of the scroll.

"I didn't know a life peer was entitled to a coat of arms," I said, stroking the stiff edge of the parchment, my fingers slipping across its silky texture. "Still, it's a beautiful work of art. Who did that for you?"

Judith allowed herself a modest smile.

"Me. Calligraphy is my hobby."

"Wow! I'm genuinely impressed."

"It's not always a blessing, though. Every summer term, just as I'm up to my ears in marking exam papers, Hairnet expects me to hand-write all the Speech Day certificates and bookplates. It takes hours."

"Still, how lovely to know that your handiwork goes out into the world in all those girls' portfolios, helping them get places at university or to land good jobs. And those prize books will forever be a source of pride to them and their descendants."

Judith brightened.

"Do you know, Gemma, I'd never thought of it like that before. Thank you, I'll bear that in mind when I'm slaving over the next batch of certificates and bookplates in July. Can you believe I have to write a hundred of each? Every girl is recognised for some form of achievement, and there is never more than one award apiece, so that no-one becomes conceited."

"How on earth does Hairnet dream up a hundred different awards?"

"Oh, there are some pretty wacky ones. Best Table Manners, Most Original Hairstyle…"

I laughed. "I bet there's stiff competition for that last one."

She smiled. "Oh yes, the girls all value any kind of recognition from old Hairnet. To be fair, some of them are the usual subject and sports prizes that you'd expect to find in any school. But she just likes to celebrate non-academic achievements too. Funnily enough, it's sometimes the winners of the more dubious awards that go on to have the most illustrious careers. Madalen, the Tidiest Bedside Table winner a few years ago, now has a flourishing business as a decluttering adviser."

Judith fetched thick hardback books from the nearest shelf and placed them on the corners of the scroll to keep it unfurled and flat.

I laughed. "Declutterer to the gentry?"

"Oh no, to ordinary people. Most clutter bugs have had some kind of trauma as a trigger to their chaotic lives. Madalen always had a wonderful way with troubled girls in her class. I can see why she's done so well."

It was heart-warming to learn of such privileged girls reaching out like this – Miss Harnett's influence, I was sure.

"But we digress." Judith tapped the scroll with a ruler that listed the dates of the kings and queens of England down one side. "You see here that Lord Bunting is recorded as having five children, all but one of whom died in babyhood."

"How very sad." I thought of his kindly face on his effigy in the mausoleum. He looked naturally paternal. "What about the one who lived longer?"

Judith tapped the fifth little line beneath Lord and Lady Bunting.

"Oliver lived to just nine years old. His death was under much different circumstances to his siblings', who all died from infections not long after birth. So common in those days, especially among the poor due to the insanitary conditions of their homes. No antibiotics, of course."

"So, what did poor Oliver die of? Was it some kind of accident?"

I could picture him having a tumble from his faithful pony, like the little girl in *Gone with the Wind*, or drowning in the lake, as in *Don't Look Now*. I shut my eyes to block out those tragic images.

"Nothing so tangible," said Judith. "Lady Bunting's diary records him going into a slow decline just after he turned eight. In Victorian times they used the word 'decline' to cover a multitude of sins, including diseases and conditions that contemporary doctors could not identify or understand."

"So, we don't really know?"

Judith hesitated.

"Actually, I think I do. Although there is no more specific diagnosis on the death certificate, I've drawn certain conclusions of my own, judging by some letters I found in the Bunting archive."

I remained silent but sat looking at her expectantly. She went on.

"In Lady Bunting's personal journal, she records her son's failure to thrive from the age of eight. Having lost several children before they were toddlers, she is hypersensitive to any adverse changes in her little boy. A good-natured, happy child with everything money could buy, he starts to lose interest in his favourite games and toys. Long after he'd left behind his routine afternoon naps, he resumes sleeping at every opportunity and starts to lose weight.

"At first, she is charmed at finding her little boy curled up like a kitten, fast asleep in a quiet corner in the middle of the day. She is also irritated by her husband's pride at his son slimming down into the proportions of a young man rather than a chubby child. It is too early for her. She is in no hurry for him to leave his childhood behind. She begins to worry."

Judith was fidgeting as she spoke, folding a scrap of paper over and over until it was too thick to bend any further. Now she paused to unfold it, pulled it out to its full extent and started the process all over again.

I tried to fill the uncomfortable pause.

"Surely even if a child slims down, they still keep growing upwards, so shouldn't lose weight?"

Judith nodded.

149

"Exactly so. Which is why Lady Bunting's maternal instincts kicked in. She called in the family physician who gave the boy a battery of tests, all inconclusive. There weren't many tests they could do in those days, not like now."

She gazed out of the window across the lawns before continuing. I knew this story did not have a happy ending, but why did it affect Judith so deeply? Why was she identifying with Lady Bunting?

"But then the boy involuntarily renders evidence of his own. During the course of the doctor's visit, he begs to be excused, not once but twice, to go to the lavatory. According to Lady Bunting's journal, at first, she refuses him permission to excuse himself, thinking it's a childish ruse to escape the doctor's attentions. The doctor intervenes on the boy's behalf, making light of his request, but she notices a wary look in his eye as the child leaves the room.

"Lady Bunting apologises profusely for the boy's rudeness, but the doctor brushes it aside, continuing with the tests on his return. When he gently presses Oliver's abdomen, the boy asks to be excused again. Before Lady Bunting can object, the good doctor rises and takes Oliver's hand, saying, 'Well done, Oliver, this gives us a chance for another test.' And with that, they leave the room."

I flinched.

"Was the doctor up to no good? I'd have been suspicious of his motives."

"Far from it. He was being exceptionally astute by the medical standards of the day. His reason for accompanying the boy was to taste his urine."

"Well, if that's not cause for maternal concern, I don't know what is!"

The very thought of it made me feel sick.

Judith clasped her hands on the tabletop.

"Yes, but not for the reasons you are thinking. The fact is, Doctor Lovett suspects he knows the cause of Oliver's decline, and the quickest way to test his theory was to apply a practice that dates back to the ancient Greeks – to taste the patient's urine to see if it's sweet."

I folded my arms.

"That sounds like some old wives' tale to me."

Judith shook her head.

"Far from it. Do you know any Greek, Gemma?"

I had to admit I didn't.

"How about French or Spanish?"

I wondered why she didn't just get to the point.

"I did French to A Level."

"OK then, *miel*. What does *miel* mean?"

"Jam. No, honey. That's right, honey."

"Spot on. In the Greek, the word for honey is very similar: *meli*. That's where the word mellitus comes from in medicine. As in *diabetes mellitus*. Diabetes means siphon – so, sweet siphon. A person with untreated Type 1 diabetes, as we call it now, is a siphon of sweet water. The body stops producing insulin, which is required to deliver sugars from the blood stream into other parts of the body to keep them functioning. High blood sugar is harmful

151

and dangerous, so the body eliminates it in the form of copious sweet urine.

"That had started to happen to Oliver, which was why he was losing so much weight. Much of the calorific value of what he was eating in his typically stodgy Victorian diet was passing straight through him in sugar water. Although eating plenty, he was undernourished and dehydrated."

The poor little soul. I felt awful now for having been suspicious of the doctor's intentions.

"But if the doctor had identified what was wrong with him, why didn't he do something about it? Why did poor Oliver die so young?"

Judith looked away, her eyes filling with tears.

"In Victorian times, there was no effective cure. Still isn't."

"But diabetics live to a ripe old age these days, don't they? My ex-boyfriend's father had it and he was in his sixties."

Judith touched her fingertips to her eyes to dispel her tears.

"There are now treatments to manage its effects, but once you get it, you've got it for life. Only in the 1920s when Sir Frederick Banting –"

"Banting? Don't you mean Bunting?" I interjected.

Judith shook her head. "No, Banting was someone completely different. No relation at all. It's just a weird coincidence. Anyway, when Banting pioneered the use of daily insulin injections, the condition was effectively commuted from a death sentence to a life sentence. That revolution came too late for young Oliver. The only course open to Victorian diabetics was to stop eating carbs."

In my head, I sorted into food groups all the things I'd eaten that day. There were a lot of carbs.

"So, a bit like the Atkins diet?" I said at last.

"Yes, but the Atkins diet wasn't devised to treat diabetics. It's used for rapid weight loss in cases of morbid obesity or in celebrities slimming down for film roles or awards ceremonies. Not for raising healthy growing children. Cutting out carbs wouldn't save Oliver's life, only prolong it slightly. But what could Lady Bunting do but embrace it? What would any mother do? The poor child's last few months must have been unbearably sad for the whole family."

Of all the things I'd expected Judith to tell me this afternoon, this was not one of them.

"How do you know all this? Lady Bunting's journal must have been very detailed."

From the archive cupboard in the corner of the library, Judith produced a slim paper pamphlet sealed in a plastic bag, the sort that archivists use to protect historical documents. She set it on the table in front of me for inspection.

"*Letter on Corpulence, Addressed to the Public* by William Banting," I read aloud. "Is that a misprint? I thought his name was Frederick, not William?"

Judith smiled for the first time since we'd sat down together.

"Sorry, it is confusing, isn't it? Still no relation to Lord Bunting and family, but a distant relative of Sir Frederick Banting. Banting's problem wasn't quite the same as

Oliver's. He had what we'd now call Type 2 diabetes, in which the body still produces insulin, but becomes less efficient at taking it up. 'Corpulence', as he termed it, is a major cause. Lose the excess weight and you can often reverse the diabetes. Not so in Type 1.

"Thanks to this pamphlet, Banting's name became a household word for the low-carb diet he adopted to slim himself down. 'Do you bant?' was a popular question in fashionable society. Or 'Are you banting?' I believe in Sweden the word *banta* is still used to mean any kind of slimming diet. The Bunting family doctor was aware of Banting, and he recommended his diet for Oliver. The poor boy could have no starch or sugar, just meat and vegetables."

"That menu wouldn't go down well with our girls, would it?"

I pictured their Halloween treats.

Judith grimaced.

"My goodness, no. It must have been torture for young Oliver and his parents too, especially when the press got hold of the story. There was a cruel cartoon parodying 'The Banting Buntings' tucking eagerly into a vast dish of salad. Not surprisingly, after the tragedy of her son's death, Lady Bunting decided she could not bear to lose any more children. She notes in her journal her decision to tell Lord Bunting further children are not an option. It is celibacy or separation. He genuinely loved his wife, so chose celibacy over separation."

We sat in silence for a few moments as I took this all in before remembering the original purpose of our conversation.

"So, no more descendants after that for Lord and Lady Bunting."

"No descendants." She leaned forward and lowered her voice. "At least, not for Lady Bunting."

"But I thought he predeceased her, and they were still married at his death?"

Judith raised her eyebrows.

"Who said anything about marriage?"

As the implications of her words sank in, I put my hands to my mouth.

"So Earl really is the illegitimate descendant of a child born out of wedlock to Lord Bunting?"

Judith picked up the pamphlet, holding the polybag carefully with her fingertips.

"His claim to be a descendant could be valid. Whether he has any rights to the estate is a separate issue. We'll come on to that in a minute."

She looked at her watch.

"But first, let's grab a cup of coffee."

She replaced the Banting pamphlet in the archive cupboard before we headed to the staffroom.

"Just one question, Judith. How do you know so much about diabetes? You're Head of History, not Head of Science."

Judith paused on the threshold of the library, her hand on the gleaming brass doorknob before turning to me with a sad smile.

"You see, the thing is, I also have Type 1 diabetes."

21

Tissue of Lies

As we strolled down the corridor to the staffroom, we caught a distant chorus of 'Hark the Herald'.

"Hadn't you wondered why whenever I accept one of Felicity's baked goods, she gives me a number?"

"I had noticed, but assumed it was a running joke between you, as if she was putting a limit on the number of items you were allowed to take."

Judith grinned as we entered the staffroom.

"No, she's telling me how many grams of carbs are in each piece. Every time I eat something, I need to know its carbohydrate content so I can give myself enough insulin for my body to process it."

She lifted the hem of her blouse to show me a small black device about the size of a packet of cigarettes clipped to the waistband of her skirt.

"My insulin pump. I wear it all the time. There's a tube attached to a cannula on my tummy, sending the insulin straight into my system."

I filled a cup for her from Old Faithful.

"Oh dear, and I took Felicity's number as licence for us to eat eight gingerbread stars each."

Judith laughed.

"Don't worry. Mavis took far more than eight, and there were still plenty to go round."

A knock on the staffroom door spared me from further admonition. Judith went to answer it while I poured a cup of coffee for myself.

"Aren't you meant to be somewhere else?" I heard Judith say. Then her voice softened. "Hang on, let me get you a tissue."

Through the open door, I could hear heartfelt sobbing. As Judith collected the box of tissues from the coffee table, she whispered, "I think she's one of yours, Gemma. Abigail Swann from Year 7."

I nodded and took the box of tissues from her.

My instinct was to draw Abigail into the seclusion of the staffroom, but an unwritten rule forbade girls entering for the sake of the teachers' privacy. Knowing the library would be empty, I put my arm round Abigail's shoulders, pressed a tissue into her hand and guided her gently in that direction. Its calm environment would be just right to soothe a sobbing girl.

I sat her down in one of the pair of fireside armchairs and perched beside her on its arm.

"So, Abigail, what has happened to upset you so much? Has one of your friends been mean to you?"

She shook her head and sniffed but said nothing.

"Which activity group have you been in this afternoon?"

Had she forgotten her lines in the nativity play? Fluffed a solo in the choir? Fallen out with her flute duet partner?

"Drama, miss. I'm being a lamb."

"That's a very important thing to be!"

She smiled weakly at my joke.

"Is your role not going well?"

Perhaps she was miffed at not having a speaking part.

She waved a handful of tissue, dismissively.

"Oh no, miss, drama's fine. I've got the best costume out of everybody. It's – it's something else."

I took the soggy tissue from her hand, threw it in the wastepaper basket and offered her the box for a fresh one.

"If you tell me what is bothering you, I expect I can help."

Abigail set her hands in her lap, her fists clenched.

"No, miss, it's far too late now. The damage is done."

"Perhaps I can help you undo it."

I hoped my expectant silence might open her up. Nothing.

"Is it something that happened in school?"

"Yes, miss," she whispered.

"Did it happen today?"

She shook her head. This was starting to feel like a game of twenty questions. I did not feel confident of winning.

"You are allowed to say more than yes or no. Tell me when it happened."

She twisted the tissue in her lap.

"It was a little while ago, miss. At the fireworks party."

I ran through that evening's schedule in my mind. What had Abigail been up to that night? Then I remembered. She was the child perched on the arm of Miss Harnett's throne.

"Oh, of course! It must have been quite a shock for you when that stray rocket whizzed straight at you out of the bonfire. Well done for your quick thinking. Everyone noticed how instantly you reacted, making Miss Harnett duck down to avoid the rocket's path. My goodness, you were brave. I don't think I'd have been as quick-witted."

She stared at me uncertainly. Further reassurance would be needed.

"Do you know, Abigail, I've a good mind to nominate you for Miss Harnett's bravery award at this year's Speech Day. You showed no fear, no thought for yourself. It was as if you'd been rehearsing for the moment of crisis, like a trained bodyguard, the sort that protects the Queen and the Prime Minister. It was almost as if you knew it was coming."

Abigail emitted a plaintive wail and dropped her face into her hands, shoulders heaving. Then I clicked. I could hardly believe what I was about to ask.

"Abigail, am I to take it that you *did* know it was coming? How could you possibly? If you saw someone plant the rocket in the bonfire, you must tell me at once so they can be punished."

I hoped to goodness it was Earl. Tangible evidence of his bad character might empower us to kick him off the premises. So far all we had were snide comments, veiled threats and bullying.

160

Abigail took a deep breath and sat up straight, hands still clenched in her lap. The tissue pressed between her fingers was by now mere papier-mâché.

"Yes, miss, you're right. I did know. I'd have known even if I'd been wearing a blindfold and had my eyes closed. Because, you see, Miss Lamb, it was me that planted that rocket."

22

Gunpowder Plot

This changed everything. Or did it? Was Abigail even telling the truth? Perhaps she was covering for someone else, namely Earl Bunting. Perhaps he had wanted to plant the rocket to intimidate Miss Harnett and bribed this poor child to do it for him, provided he could muster the cash for once.

"I can't believe it, Abigail. Why on earth would you launch a rocket at Miss Harnett? I thought you loved her. We all do."

Abigail wiped her tears away on the sleeve of her jumper.

"Oh, but I do love Miss Harnett, Miss Lamb, I do. The thing is, this was the first St Bride's bonfire party that we'd been to, so we didn't know that's where Miss Harnett always sits for the fireworks. We didn't work that out till later. We thought that big chair had been put there for the Earl. All of us Year 7s did. We thought he'd be sitting on the throne because he's the school's special guest and he's an Earl. We don't love the Earl, not at all. Even if he is Lord Bunting's grandson. The Earl – that's who we were aiming for."

I bit my lip, inwardly applauding her inventiveness. She must have sneaked the rocket into the bonfire when the others were either desecrating or cleaning Earl's car – the perfect distraction for anyone passing by, and for all the staff watching out of the staffroom window. My goodness, she had pluck!

"That's no excuse, Abigail. You know directing a firework at a person is deeply wrong. You could have blinded him or left him horribly disfigured. Weren't you listening to Mr Security's firework safety talk in assembly that morning?"

Abigail gazed into the fire, unable to look me in the eye.

"Yes, miss, of course we were. That's what gave us the idea. Our very own gunpowder plot!"

"*We?*" I queried, only just cottoning on to the significance of the plural pronoun. "*Our* own gunpowder plot? Who do you mean by 'we'?"

Abigail chewed her lips, obviously wrestling with her conscience while deciding whether to rat on her friends.

"All the other Year 7s in my dorm," she said at last. "On the morning of the bonfire party, when we saw the throne out there, we decided it would be a good way to drive that horrible Earl away. We don't want him living in the school. We don't even like him being a visitor. But we didn't mean to hurt him, just to frighten him off."

I struggled for words to defend Earl.

"That's beside the point, Abigail. No matter who was sitting in that chair, it would still have been a dreadful thing to do. And as for poor Miss Harnett, I can't think of a less deserving victim for such a horrible prank."

For the first time, Abigail looked me in the eye.

"But that's exactly why they sent me to guard Miss Harnett. It was only when she arrived at the bonfire party that we realised the throne wasn't for the Earl. By then it was too late for us to be able to remove the rocket from the bonfire. So, the others sent me to protect Miss Harnett when the rocket took off. I was ready to save her, even if it meant sacrificing myself."

"Who gave you the dangerous task of throwing yourself in the path of the rocket?"

She wrinkled her nose.

"The others decided I'd be best at it because out of all of us, I am the biggest scaredy cat. That meant I'd be most likely to get away with sitting by Miss Harnett for comfort. Someone like Imogen couldn't have done it. She'd have to act being anxious, and she's rubbish at acting. You should see her in the nativity play, miss, you'd never believe she is really a donkey."

I sighed. Managing the girls had been almost trouble-free for me since I'd joined the school. I'd never had to issue so much as a detention. A gently sarcastic reprimand, delivered without a smile, had always been enough to keep them in check. I thought it had seemed too good to be true.

I had no idea how to deal with a misdemeanour of this magnitude. Should I escalate it straight away to the highest authority in the school, Miss Harnett? I played for time.

"If you've all been in this together, I think it's only fair that you should be punished together too. You need to learn from this before you move on. Are the others involved as upset as you are?"

I hadn't noticed any remorseful girls moping about, but maybe they were all better actors than Imogen.

Abigail shook her head.

"No, miss, I'm the only one who's this upset. My grandma says I'm a sensitive flower."

I pursed my lips to suppress a smile.

"You're also the one who took the greatest risk, Abigail."

Silent tears began to flow down her flushed cheeks. I longed to make her feel better without making light of her crime.

"But you showed bravery, Abigail, both in protecting Miss Harnett at grave risk to yourself and in confessing what you did. We'll say no more about it today. Let's not disrupt the important preparations for the charity Christmas Fair. But I shall speak to Miss Harnett tomorrow, and you will have to explain your appalling behaviour to her. She will decide the best way for you to make amends."

"Yes, Miss Lamb."

Gazing up at me from under her damp eyelashes, Abigail took a final sniff before getting up to leave.

"Now, off you go, back to your rehearsal. And, Abigail?"

"Yes, miss?"

"Do you know what my grandma used to say to me whenever I had a crisis when I was your age?"

"No, miss."

"That it was character-building. Deal with this in the right way and you'll come out the other side of the crisis a better, stronger person."

As she pondered that message, I realised it also applied to what I'd been through with Steven.

"Now, run along."

With a watery smile, she skipped out through the door. I was just congratulating myself on how well I'd handled the situation when I heard a shriek from her direction, followed by the speedy patter of school shoes charging across the hall's parquet floor. Next thing I knew, Earl strode into the library, a self-satisfied smile on his face.

I hoped to goodness he hadn't been listening at the door.

23

Hereditary Rights and Wrongs

Earl was clutching a pile of photographs in one hand.

"Hi there, Miss Limp, and good afternoon to you."

A simple hello would have sufficed.

He gestured towards the archive cupboard in the corner.

"I've just come to deposit these old snapshots. In the school archive, not the family one."

On his way, he paused at the table on which Judith had spread out the Bunting family tree. Setting the photos down, he reached inside his jacket and pulled out his gold pen. It baffled me why he had to dress so formally all the time. Perhaps he hadn't brought any informal clothes with him from the States. Perhaps he didn't possess any. Which was odd, because I thought Americans dressed more casually than we British. Or maybe his casual clothes were being shipped over along with his fleet of luxury cars.

Having stooped to pick up a few shreds of Abigail's damp tissue and put them in the wastepaper basket, I reached the table just too late to stop him uncapping his pen and drawing a sideways line in green ink from Lord Bunting's name to a blank space beside it. When I saw his crooked addition to Judith's meticulous calligraphy, I wanted to slap him.

"Earl, no! What on earth are you doing?"

He gave a condescending smile.

"Why, updating the family tree, of course. There's a significant branch missing, starting with my pioneering ancestor, Mary O'Flaherty."

He continued to write on the parchment, adding more lines and names beneath Mary's. Although his handwriting was large and bold, its loops were so tightly closed that no-one would be able to read what he'd written.

"But it must have taken Judith hours and hours to draw it up. You can't just deface it to suit yourself. You have no right."

He paused to raise an eyebrow at me.

"I have plenty of rights, Miss Lamb. Hereditary rights. You're an English teacher. Surely you know the meaning of hereditary?"

When I refused to dignify his question with a reply, he carried on regardless.

"As a history teacher, Judith Duckling needs to improve the accuracy of her record-keeping."

The last name he wrote was of course his own. Then he recapped his pen and threw it down on the table, tempting me to pick it up and cross out his additions, while he went to stuff the pile of photos into the school section of the archive cupboard.

"So long, Miss Limb, and good day to you."

Touching a forefinger to his temple in salute, he headed for the door.

Too angry to speak, I stood staring at his scrawl. Might Judith blame me for letting him deface her document?

I found out soon enough. There was a gentle tap at the door, Judith tactfully checking before entering for the sake of Abigail's dignity.

"Come in, Judith, please."

At the despair in my voice, Judith rushed over to join me, bringing the remains of our coffees.

"Did you manage to sort Abigail – oh!"

Catching sight of the defaced family tree, she nearly dropped our drinks.

"Who on earth?"

Then she spotted Earl's distinctive golden pen with which he had inadvertently incriminated himself.

"That wretched Earl Bunting! How dare he? Does he know how long that calligraphy took me?"

"I tried to tell him, but he wouldn't listen. He started scrawling on it before I could stay his hand."

"Does he realise how much parchment cost? That's top-of-the-range stuff. It's very expensive."

She set down the coffee cups and grabbed his pen.

"Right, I'm confiscating his precious fountain pen as revenge. I've a good mind to sell it to cover the cost of the parchment."

I was glad to be able to help with that, at least by proxy.

"Ask Joe to do that for you. He's got an eBay account. He's been using it to sell off old school sports kit. We can ask him about it tomorrow."

After raising the parchment to the light to check Earl's ink was dry, Judith rolled it up and returned it to its protective tube. When she went to replace it in the cupboard, I remembered Earl's other addition to the archive.

"Earl just stuffed a pile of photos in there. He reckoned they belonged with the school's documents, not the family's, so I don't know why he had them."

Judith sighed.

"I don't think I can bear to look at them just now, Gemma. Come on, let's go and watch a bit of the nativity play rehearsal to cheer ourselves up. It's always good for a laugh."

"Great idea. The photos can wait until tomorrow. After all, isn't that the point of an archive – to be there for ever more?"

24

Pengate

After lunch the following day, wanting to keep our eBay plan a secret from the rest of the staffroom, Judith and I went to speak to Joe in private.

"I presume his sale of school sports kit is official," said Judith as we headed for the pavilion, where Joe had gone to do a few chores before afternoon lessons.

"I'm pretty sure it is. Otherwise I don't think he'd have told me about it."

After the morning's drizzle, the grass on the playing fields was wet underfoot, splashing my tights as far up as my knees. It might have been a better idea to ask Joe to meet us in my classroom, but I was interested to see inside his pavilion, which I'd never visited before.

As we climbed the shallow wooden steps to the low verandah, the creaking of the boards under our hard-soled shoes heralded our arrival. Even so, I knocked on the door rather than barging in. Privacy and solitude are highly

173

prized at St Bride's. Outside of lesson time, the pavilion would be a useful bolthole for Joe if he wanted to be alone.

From within came a strange scraping sound that I couldn't identify. I wondered what he got up to in there.

"It's only me, Joe," I called. "And Miss Gosling. No girls with us."

The scraping sound ceased, to be followed by the clunk of wood on wood, perhaps a cricket bat being thrown on to the floor. Then the door swung open and Joe, with a piece of dusty sandpaper in his hand, was greeting me with a big smile before turning it on Judith.

"Good afternoon, ladies. Have you come to offer me a sporting challenge?"

I wrinkled my nose. "Are there any sports that can be played between three people? I can't think of any."

Joe grinned.

"Don't worry, I'm not going to insult you by suggesting a two against one match. I wouldn't dare. But we could play a round of golf together, if you fancy it?"

"Not at the end of November, thanks," said Judith. "I'm a fair-weather golfer."

"Me too," I added quickly, despite having no idea how to play. If it turned out he was keen on golf, perhaps I might ask Joe to teach me. I'd never considered a round of golf an agreeable pastime until now.

"Is your visit extra-curricular?" he asked, beckoning us to join him inside. His shady den was redolent of polish or resin or whatever it is you treat sports equipment with. Those chemicals must become overwhelming after a while. No wonder the windows at the front were ajar to keep fresh air circulating, even on this chilly November afternoon.

In the far corner, at a forty-five-degree angle to the walls, stood an ancient, its chintz cover coated in a layer of fine dust. The same residue covered the front of Joe's mauve tracksuit trousers and trainers. Beside the chair stood a low oak coffee table with a touch of Art Deco in its design, and on top was a wooden hockey stick.

Joe laid the sandpaper down beside the stick and pulled a couple of folding slatted wooden chairs out from behind the armchair. He opened them up to allow us to sit down, then resumed his seat in the armchair. Then he picked up the wooden hockey stick and began scraping the sandpaper back and forth across the lettering that proclaimed the school's ownership.

Judith looked at me, as if hoping I'd explain our mission.

"We've come to ask a favour," I began. "You see, Earl damaged Judith's property yesterday, and we want to exact revenge."

Joe stopped sanding and raised his eyebrows.

"You want me to damage him?" He lifted the hockey stick from his lap and swung it through the air like a sword. "Sorry, GBH isn't my style. Besides, I'm sure it must go against even Hairnet's lenient school rules."

Judith touched my arm to indicate she wanted to take over.

"To be fair, Joe, it wasn't really my property. It belongs to the school, but I put a lot of hard work into it. Do you remember a couple of years ago, Hairnet asked me to draw up the Bunting family tree?"

Joe grinned.

"Yes, wasn't it part of a school-wide project for the girls to study their own family history?"

Judith nodded.

"Yes, and wasn't that a fascinating piece of prep to mark?"

Chuckling, Joe turned to me.

"Shame you missed it, Gemma. Those family trees did the rounds in the staffroom. Absolutely amazing, some of them, not to mention scandalous."

Judith smiled.

"I'd originally planned to let the girls take them home at the end of the summer term, but Max asked me to keep them in school in the interests of security. I knew a few girls had notable parents but tucked away in some of their family trees are minor royalty and major celebrities. The tabloids would have had a field day if they'd got hold of those connections."

"Anyway, back to the subject," I interjected to spare Joe any further reminder of the powers of the more scurrilous press. "You were telling me the other day that you'd been flogging off some old sports kit on eBay."

"With the Bursar's blessing, I'll have you know."

He brandished the hockey stick in mock defence.

"I've finally managed to persuade him to invest in some new carbon fibre sticks so we can ditch these old wooden ones. They are positively antique. No-one plays with wooden sticks anymore. So I've been putting them on eBay. The proceeds are helping to pay for new replacements."

I reached out to touch the stick in his hand, running my finger along the pale, even rectangle of bare, clean wood from which the school's name had all but vanished.

"But if no-one plays with wooden sticks these days, how come you are able to sell them? Surely no-one wants to buy them?"

Joe brushed some sawdust off the surface before resuming his sanding.

"You'd be surprised what people buy on eBay. One man's meat and all that. Money for old rope, if you'll excuse the double helping of clichés, Miss Lamb."

He'd heard me scold the girls for overuse of clichés, although just as often they surprised me with their original expressions.

"It's true, though," he continued. "If you go on to eBay and put 'old rope' in the search box, you'll find loads of it for sale. Makes me think I'm in the wrong job."

"Does the same go for wooden hockey sticks?"

"You betcha. They get snapped up – well, not literally – by interior designers kitting out sports-themed pubs."

"I knew pubs did that with books. There's a place down in Somerset, the Bookbarn, where you can buy books by the metre."

"You've obviously been going to the wrong sort of pubs," Joe teased. "Is this your roundabout way of asking me to sell some old books for you? I thought that Mavis Brook had that gig taped."

"Not books, but pens. Or rather, a pen." I couldn't resist a smug smile. "Earl Bunting's pen, to be precise."

Joe laughed.

"What, that fancy gold one he keeps flashing about? Probably came as a gift set with his watch and chain. Accessories for the Pretentious, by appointment to Earl Bunting."

Judith produced her pencil case from her book bag and unzipped it to pull out Earl's pen. The engraving on the barrel showed up better in the dim light of the sports pavilion than it had in the big-windowed library. But when she dropped it into Joe's open palm, it landed with the inscription facing down.

"I'm sure there'll be a huge demand for posh pens on eBay," he began. "Lots of people collect vintage stationery, and plenty more love stationery of any kind. Although it might be harder to shift a pen bearing Earl's personal inscription on it. There can't be many other Earl Buntings out there, and I can hardly sand down solid gold."

When Joe turned the pen over to read the inscription, he broke out into a gale of laughter.

"Do you reckon this is his middle name?" He held it up to show us. "Earl Sample Not for Sale Bunting?"

"Oh, my word!" cried Judith, peering at it in the dim light. "Do you know, I didn't even think to read the inscription. I just hid it in my pencil case as fast as I could." She sighed. "Now I know it's not a family heirloom treasured down the generations, I feel much better about flogging it."

"But he might be Earl Sample Not for Sale Bunting III," said Joe. "For all we know, his grandfather was the first holder of that illustrious name."

Laughing, I took the pen from Joe's outstretched palm.

"Stupid of him to leave it lying around where anyone could read it. It does rather undermine his claim to the estate."

"Not that a pen with the right name on it would prove his claim," said Judith. "Anyone can get a pen engraved. I've got one a child gave me saying 'World's Best Teacher'. Doesn't make it true. What matters is the will."

Joe pulled a duster from his trouser pocket to give a final wipe to the hockey stick. Then he held it up to show us.

"There! One anonymous hockey stick. Now I can post it on eBay. I'm under strict instructions from the Bursar not to bring the school into disrepute by selling off named possessions."

"No, only he's allowed to do that," added Judith, bitterly. "Talk about double standards. He seems to think selling the family silver improves the school's public image by suggesting it's a classy joint, as if the world at large will assume the Ming vase or whatever is just surplus to requirements."

I wondered whether the Bursar had anything else valuable left to sell.

"Do you still want me to flog Earl's pen for you?" Joe asked eventually.

Judith bit her lip.

"Satisfying though that might be, now that I've seen the dubious inscription, I'm thinking it might be better to hang on to it as evidence. It may prove useful, though I'm not sure how."

I pretended to be shocked.

"Surely you don't mean to blackmail him, Miss Gosling?"

She grinned.

"No, but we might have some fun with it."

The way things were going this term, I thought we could all do with a bit more fun.

25

Photo Finish

"My photos! Who's taken my photos?"

Flushed and sweating, the Bursar burst into the staffroom.

Oriana looked up from the window-seat, where she was engrossed in the latest issue of *Hello* magazine.

"Seen an unflattering shot of yourself in here? Which page? I'll look it up."

"I wouldn't have put you down as camera shy, Bursar," said Mavis, cramming a whole gingerbread star into her mouth.

"Let me get you a coffee, Bursar," offered Joe, patting him on the shoulder in moral support. Without waiting for an answer, Joe poured a cup, added milk and sugar, and passed it over to him. St Bride's staffroom coffee is like penicillin. Taken in moderation, it's a powerful fix for many ills.

With his free hand, the Bursar pulled a large white linen handkerchief from his pocket to mop his brow.

"Not photos of me, you fools."

"Bit harsh, Bursar," said Judith, a natural peacemaker.

The Bursar seemed too agitated to speak. Then I remembered the pile of photos Earl had stashed in the archive cupboard. I hadn't yet looked at them, but they might have been what he was looking for. I was glad to come to the Bursar's rescue.

"Whoever they're of, Bursar, I think I may know where they are now."

The Bursar bounded towards me, so wired even before he'd drunk his coffee that I felt almost under attack. I held my hands up in front of me in defence.

"Not that I took them from your study. But I think I know who did."

His shaking hands slopped coffee from his cup into its saucer. I took a step back, not wanting brown spatters down my cream cardigan.

"Who? Who took them? Tell me, Gemma, please."

"Drink your coffee and I'll take you to see them, and you can check whether they're the ones you're looking for."

The Bursar took a comforting swig from his trembling cup.

"Did you look at the pictures?"

I wondered why that thought made him nervous.

"No, not at all. I was just watching from the other side of the room when Earl put a pile of old snaps in the archive cupboard."

He returned his empty cup to the trolley and followed me out of the room.

We passed beneath the all-seeing gaze of Lord Bunting's portrait, dodging little huddles of girls enjoying a leisurely chat in the brief interlude between supper and evening prep. The Bursar was muttering in a low voice, as much to himself as to me.

"Why Earl has to take everything from my office rather than letting me collect my possessions myself is a mystery. He's just adding insult to injury."

His rage was making him walk far faster than usual, and I had to hasten my step to keep up with him.

"Why on earth is he taking stuff from your study at all? He's not stealing, is he?" I was determined to catch Earl red-handed at something. Theft would do nicely. "If we have proof –"

Then I broke off, remembering Earl's gold pen in Judith's book bag. Pot, kettle.

"He's taken over my study, Gemma. He's taking all I've got. First my home, now my workplace. What next?"

The Bursar looked so bereft that I thought he might cry. We entered the sanctuary of the library not a moment too soon.

"The sneaky beggar announced to me this morning that he'd usurped my study as a *fait accompli*. Somehow he got in there yesterday without so much as a by-your-leave."

"But you always keep it locked, Bursar, what with all the girls' confidential records in there, plus the petty cash. If he's breaking and entering, surely we can report him to the police and get him out of here that way? He might have rights to the estate, but not to items belonging to the school, or to your personal property."

The Bursar stuffed his hands into his trouser pockets and shuffled his feet like a naughty schoolboy caught raiding the tuck shop.

"Please don't tell a soul, Gemma, but a few days ago I mislaid the key to my study and haven't been able to lock it since."

"Mislaid it? Or do you think Earl stole it?"

The Bursar shrugged.

"I've no idea, but I didn't lose any sleep over it. I just assumed I'd dropped it somewhere, and that someone would find it and return it to my pigeonhole. It has one of those big old brass school tags on it saying 'Bursary' just for that purpose. Whenever I've lost it before, the finder has always returned it straight away. It never occurred to me that our little cuckoo might launch a raid on my study while I was off visiting my mother on Sunday. But when I came down from that wretched butler's flat this morning, there he was, bold as brass, sitting in my chair with his feet up on my desk."

The poor Bursar. As if he hadn't already suffered enough.

"What about the petty cash?"

"Oh, he'd emptied that on Friday, when he made me pay his weekly allowance. Why can't the man get a bank account? If our girls can do it, so can he."

As part of Essential Life Skills, Felicity Button teaches new girls during their first term how to open a bank account and reconcile their balances.

"I bet his allowance hasn't even covered his bar bill."

The Bursar's voice went up an octave.

"His bar bill, Gemma? Since when has there been a staff bar? Why haven't I been invited? Goodness knows, I could do with a stiff Scotch right now."

He slumped down in an armchair by the fire as I headed for the archive cupboard.

"Not a school bar, Bursar. A pub one. The Bluebird in Wendlebury Barrow. I went there for lunch during exeat and Donald, the publican, said Earl was running up quite a tab there."

"Really? A tab carried over from one visit to the next? Donald's never let me do that. Mind you, I'd never even think of asking for one. Donald struggles to keep that pub open even with people paying on the spot. He can't afford to offer free credit."

"Earl's posh car did the trick, apparently. Donald assumed he must be loaded to drive a Rolls-Royce."

"Didn't we all?" There was bitterness in the Bursar's voice as he held out his hands to receive the pile of photos. "That's part of the trouble. He does things that no-one else would dream of trying to get away with, yet never quite breaks the law. Goodness knows, Gemma, if I could have found a legal excuse to oust him from St Bride's before now, I'd have done so. But unfortunately, every step he takes is backed up by the paperwork he brought with him. What he showed the governors convinced them of his title to the property. And so we're stuck with him. Anyway, please show me the photographs, Gemma."

It was an unruly pile. Some photos were clinging together due to the strips of still-tacky sticky tape at their corners; others had blobs of grey adhesive on their backs.

It looked as if Earl had torn them down from a display board. The corners had been ripped right off a few pictures.

As the Bursar sorted through the pile, the familiar image on the top reminded me where I'd seen them before: inside the cupboard door in his study. I'd seen them there only once, by chance and from a distance, in the first half of term. I'd just left a meeting in his office when I had to return for something I'd left behind. Already late for my next lesson, I'd barged back into his study unannounced as he was opening the cupboard. There on the inside of the door, like fan pictures in a schoolboy's locker, had been a fine array of photographs of Oriana.

26

Snapped Up

Except they weren't. The likeness to Oriana was remarkable, and as I had only ever seen them from the other side of the Bursar's study, it was an easy mistake to make. The fact that the woman in the photos was dressed in 1980s and 1990s fashions had seemed perfectly reasonable at the time. Oriana often wore vintage clothing.

When I'd first glimpsed his photo gallery, I'd assumed the Bursar had a massive crush on Oriana. The revelation had made me uncomfortable, because he was about twice her age. Joe had set me straight on that score. Before half term, he told me the Bursar loves Oriana like a daughter. It made me feel quite sorry for him; in his lonely bachelor existence, his only close companion is his mother, whom he visits in Cheltenham on his days off.

But now I saw the photos at close quarters, I realised my error. They were unmistakeably of Miss Harnett, taken when she was about the same age as Oriana is now. Having seen Oriana occasionally *au naturel*, I could tell at once that her resemblance to a young Miss Harnett was striking. I was surprised I hadn't noticed it before. Perhaps that was another reason for Oriana's chameleon tendencies – she didn't want anyone to spot the family likeness? Only Joe, the Bursar and I know they are mother and daughter.

I wondered whether Earl, finding the photos, had also misread the Bursar's crush, rejoicing at another useful source of blackmail material. I wondered whether he'd kept copies of the pictures. No wonder he was able to bend the Bursar so easily to his will. If Miss Harnett ever found out about the Bursar's feelings for her, she would be horrified – and quite possibly he would lose his job.

"Don't worry, Bursar," I said, patting the hand that clutched the photos. "I understand. We all love Miss Harnett. Your secret's safe with me."

He turned puppy dog eyes on me.

"That's very kind of you, Gemma. In a way it's a relief that the cat's out of the bag. But please keep it to yourself."

"Yes, of course," I replied.

Hugging the photos to his chest, the Bursar lowered his eyes.

"You see, there are other things Earl Bunting knows about me that would close the school down if he revealed them. Why do you think I've rolled over and given in to his every demand, no matter how unreasonable? Hijacking my study is the last straw…"

The Bursar could not have looked more dejected.

"Surely you can't do your job without access to your study?"

"Oh, he knows that. He moved all my papers into the old butler's office next door to the flat where I've been living ever since he commandeered my house. He said that should do me just as well."

"So, it's not without historical precedent if it used to be a study."

"That's no consolation, Gemma. It's a tiny cubicle of a room. All the butler used it for was to keep the wages records and pay the staff. My job is far more complex and responsible, yet now I'm supposed to do it in an office the size of the box Miss Harnett uses to take McPhee to the vet. It's hardly suitable for a man in my position."

I tried again to lift his spirits.

"Well, perhaps you could cheer yourself up by sticking your photos on the wall of your new office."

He ran his fingers through his thinning hair.

"I don't think so, Gemma. That's the point. I don't want to display them where everyone can see them. I can't bear it that Earl even knows about them."

Did Miss Harnett also know about them? I didn't like to ask.

"I promise I won't tell a soul, Bursar."

I hoped our new intimacy might persuade him to tell me what other secrets Earl had up his sleeve, but no such luck. After a few minutes' silence, I gave up.

"Anyway, you've got your photos back now. That's the main thing."

Briefly he lowered his guard. His voice sounded wistful.

"You know, I took most of these photos myself, back in the day."

He held one up to show me Miss Harnett in an impeccable Thatcheresque power suit, a large diamanté leopard pinned to her shoulder. She must have been no more than 30.

"I bought her that brooch, knowing how much she loves cats. It was a modern copy of one of the Duchess of Windsor's. Well, 1980s, anyway." He gazed unseeingly through the window that gave on to the lawns. "That must seem like ancient history to a young woman like you, Gemma."

"I suppose you must have been at St Bride's as long as Miss Harnett?"

His eyes came back into focus and he looked at me directly.

"Oh, yes. And as to Oriana –" He knew I knew Oriana was Miss Harnett's daughter "– I've known Oriana since before she was born."

"How lovely."

I kept my voice gentle. It must have been difficult for him to see the woman he loved bear another man's child, especially by a philandering married governor. We all had our reasons for staying faithful to St Bride's. The Bursar's was the most poignant I'd come across so far.

27

New Order

The Christmas carols echoing around the school for the last few weeks of term lifted all our spirits. Goodness knows, we needed it. By that time, Earl had managed to annoy just about everyone on the staff with his snide remarks and sense of entitlement. Thankfully he visited the staffroom less often these days, because whenever he did, Oriana would descend on him, attempting to insinuate herself into his affections.

She was trying her best not to be put off, but his tactless rejection made me cross on her behalf.

"Perhaps he just doesn't fancy girls," I suggested gently, after Earl had been particularly abrupt with her one morning during break. "He's not worthy of you, anyway." Oriana didn't reply, but she must have known that. If it wasn't for her desire to keep the St Bride's estate in her family, I doubt she'd have given him a second glance.

That evening, I happened to get Oriana alone in our House sitting room after seeing the girls safely into bed. The shelves of books and DVDs had become very jumbled, and Oriana and I had agreed that we'd spend half an hour putting them straight. In any case, we wanted the sitting room to look its best ready for the girls to put up Christmas decorations the following weekend.

However, we couldn't agree on what constituted 'best'. Oriana, so obsessed with appearances, was all for arranging the books by the colour of their spines. As an English teacher, I was lobbying for alphabetical order by author. In the end, I gave way to her argument that a rainbow arrangement would look prettier for the festivities. In return, she promised that if I wanted to reorganise them my way at the start of the spring term, I had her permission. It seemed fair enough. After all, she was Housemistress and I was only her deputy.

We began our task by taking all the books off the shelves and sorting them into piles by colour on the floor. Working together on a task that precluded us from eye contact provided the perfect opportunity for me to press her about Earl. I was torn between wanting to persuade her to give up on him and longing to hear that he had been much nicer to her when they were on their own.

I approached the subject with care.

"Will you be spending the Christmas holidays on site?"

She placed the last red book on the shelf and stood back to admire our handiwork so far.

"We usually do, Mum and me, although we keep to her suite of rooms. The Bursar turns the central heating off in

192

the rest of the building to save money, the wretch. I only go back to my flat to sleep."

Ever since my conversation with the Bursar about his photos, I'd found myself increasingly sympathetic to him. I scooped up an armful of orange books, mostly old Penguins, and brought them over to her.

"That must save a fortune. Does the Bursar stay here at Christmas too? I gather his mum's in a care home, so I don't suppose he can stay with her."

She looked at me as if I was insane.

"Of course not."

She started placing the orange books on the shelf. There were many more orange than red.

"He usually tries to inveigle an invitation, but always ends up going to visit his mother on Christmas Day until Boxing Day. And when we do see him, he goes back to Honeysuckle Lodge to sleep."

I started opening the yellow books in turn, banging them shut to shift the dust.

"Anyone else join you at school for the holidays? I should think your family would be itching for an invitation to spend the festive season in such a beautiful setting. It would be like a traditional country-house Christmas party."

Oriana got up off the floor to fetch scissors and sticky tape to repair a ripped Gerald Durrell. She positioned the ripped cover against the spine, then I held the book in place while she applied the tape.

"We don't really have any close relations. Why, are you hinting, Gemma? Do you want to stay in school too? I thought you were going to your parents straight after the end of term?"

"No, I'm definitely spending the whole holiday with my parents. I'm still making up for lost time. I was just thinking how empty the building must feel here with just the two of you."

I turned my attention to the shelf full of red books. Oriana was right. Her approach was far prettier. I reordered it by shades of red, to create a subtle gradation within the block of colour.

Oriana shrugged.

"It does feel like a completely different place in the absence of staff and girls. But you've experienced that yourself, haven't you, when you've stayed in school during exeats? Is Joe going with you to your parents?"

I tried to sound light and causal.

"Oh no, we're nowhere near the stage of meeting each other's parents. At least that's one problem you don't have to worry about. Your mother met your boyfriend before you did."

Oriana dropped the scissors and stared at me, suddenly radiant.

"Oh Gemma, do you really think of Earl as my boyfriend? I'm not at all sure he sees things that way. I mean, we've been out for meals and drinks and things, and of course I've had to take up swimming big time as he's so keen."

She ruffled her hair with her fingertips.

"The chlorine's playing havoc with the condition of my hair. It's lost all its body."

Her thick straight hair had certainly lost its usual sheen, an ever-present feature whatever colour she dyed it.

"I'll tell you something else that swimming with Earl has made me notice. He's much fonder of swimming than I am. By the time he's ready to leave, my fingertips are like prunes and I'm shivering with cold, desperate to restore myself with a hot shower. So I'm always first out of the water. This means that for once, I'm looking down on him, at the top of his head, as he climbs up the ladder to get out of the pool. I know this may sound an unfair criticism coming from me but having seen his hair all wet and slicked down flat, I've come to the conclusion that Earl is not a natural brunette. His hair is not like Lord Bunting's in the portrait at all. His roots are 100% auburn. Honestly, Gemma, is that what I'm reduced to in my quest to save the school? Dating a man who dyes his hair?"

In my astonishment at her unusual candour and her audacious double standards, I shoved an indigo book among the orange. Oriana immediately snatched it back off the shelf, tutting.

"Are you sure it's not grey or white?" I asked. "A lot of men like to keep their youthful hair colour as they age these days."

Oriana gave me an old-fashioned look.

"Gemma, trust me. I know a genuine hair colour when I see one. Earl Bunting is a redhead."

28

The Red-Headed League

While Oriana's concern about Earl's hair dye was to do with her self-esteem, mine was more about its impact on his claim to be Lord Bunting's heir. At the earliest opportunity next day, I buttonholed Dr Fleming, the science teacher, for advice.

After lunch, we strolled down to the mausoleum together, where I thought we'd be guaranteed more privacy than in the main school building. As soon as we were on our own, I started to grill her.

"If Earl Bunting has red hair, does this mean he can't be a true descendant of Lord Bunting? He had very dark hair. Apart from the portrait in the hall, I've seen pictures of him in the archive cupboard. I thought dark-haired parents couldn't have redheaded descendants."

Dr Fleming opened the gate to the walled enclosure around the mausoleum.

"That's a popular myth, Gemma. They can if they both carry a recessive gene for red hair."

I heaved open the old oak door and allowed her to go first. This was the first time I'd entered the mausoleum since the unfortunate incident there in the first half of term. Returning made me anxious.

"You're correct to think hair colour is genetically determined, but it's not that straightforward. Each parent has a pair of hair colour genes. These may both be brunette, or red or blond, or they may be two different ones – a brunette and a blond, say. Brunette is always dominant. But offspring inherit one hair colour gene from each parent, and it's the combination of two inherited genes, rather than the actual hair colour of the parents, that determines the child's hair."

We strolled towards Lord Bunting's effigy to pat him on the shoulder in greeting. Strange how we all felt a certain family loyalty towards him, yet Earl, who looked so much like him and claimed to be related, seemed alien.

"So, what you're saying is that the child of two brunette parents may turn out to be something other than brunette. Provided both parents have a blond or red-haired gene, and the child inherits two blond or two red-haired genes, he could be a blond or a redhead. But if he inherits one brunette gene from either of them, he will definitely be brunette."

"Exactly, Gemma. I wish my Year 9s would latch on to genetics that fast."

I settled down on one of the velvet chairs set against the wall for visitors.

"It's a shame, though."

Dr Fleming came to sit beside me.

"What makes you say that? Don't you like redheads?"

I laughed.

"Of course I do. And blonds and brunettes and everything else."

"How did you find out about his natural hair colour, anyway?"

"Oriana told me. She's noticed when they've been swimming, and his hair's all wet and slicked down, that he's got auburn roots."

"I can't say I've noticed, but hair dye is one of Oriana's special subjects, so I'll take her word on that. He must touch up the colour at night when no-one's looking. He's probably taking it for granted that Oriana's not going to rat on him. She's about the only member of staff on his side and the only one who will care about his vanity."

"It's not his vanity that bothers me. I'd just got my hopes up that if he had red hair, it might disprove his claim to be descended from Lord Bunting."

"Sorry to disappoint you, Gemma. Besides, at the end of the day, it doesn't matter whether his hair's naturally purple, green, or sky-blue-pink. According to the Bursar, he's showed the governors the paperwork to prove his claim."

I sighed. "Oh well, it was worth a try."

"Anyway, I'm afraid I must dash back to my lab now. I've just got time before next lesson to set up the complex apparatus I need for my demonstration for Year 12s."

Feeling more at ease in the mausoleum now, I lingered behind to take stock of the facts. Having a free period next lesson, I was in no hurry to leave. All I could prove against

Earl so far was the possible theft of a pen. Even that he might have come by honestly, perhaps as a brand ambassador, or, further down the pecking order, as a pen salesman in an upmarket department store. Neither of these scenarios negated his claim to the St Bride's estate.

I circled the plinth a couple of times, looking at Lord Bunting from all angles, willing him to inspire me, as he did Miss Harnett on her frequent visits. He didn't let me down. For the first time, I noticed the difference between the portrait and the effigy. Obviously, one was full colour and the other pure cream alabaster. But that was immaterial. The effigy had an extra dimension that until now I had not considered.

Sherlock Holmes once said that you cannot disguise a back. Now I realised that neither can you disguise a profile. Earl Bunting may have modelled his appearance on the portrait in the hall, conveniently prompted by my predecessor, and he'd done a remarkably fine job, down to the cut of his moustache and the length of his watch chain. But no matter what he did to his hair, his moustache, or his outfits, he could never pass for Lord Bunting in three dimensions. Short of plastic surgery, he would be unable to change the side view of his brow, his nose and his chin, all quite different to those of the real Lord Bunting, who continued to sleep peacefully beneath his lifelike effigy.

29

Watching Brief

No wonder Earl had resisted all invitations to visit the mausoleum with Oriana or anyone else. He had prior knowledge of the effigy from the photo my predecessor had shared online. He knew all along that when seen in three dimensions he was much less similar to Lord Bunting than when compared to the portrait.

The discovery left me spoiling for a fight with Earl, who I was now convinced was an imposter. I was therefore delighted to almost bump into him when I returned to the school building. I found him in a state of disarray, tearing down the corridor towards the staffroom, as I approached from the garden door.

"Well, hallelujah, if it isn't Miss Lump! Where do all you teachers hide yourselves when I need you?"

"In classrooms, Earl. This is a seat of learning, in case you've forgotten, and it's lesson time. You've only found me now because I happen to have a free period. Which I believe is about to end and take me from you."

This was my best chance so far to test another of my theories about Earl's subterfuge. I glanced at my wrist as if to check the time on my watch. I never wear a watch in school as there are clocks in every classroom and the staffroom, and a reliable system of bells to mark key moments in the school day.

"Oh, bother, I forgot to put my watch on this morning. If you can tell me the time, I can tell you whether I have a sufficiently long interval to help you solve whatever your problem is."

I smiled sweetly.

"What? Oh, I don't know. I never wear a wristwatch either. I'm a gentleman of leisure, not a slave to the school timetable."

Manipulative flirting doesn't come naturally to me, but I reached out playfully to tug gently on the familiar gold watch chain looped from his buttonhole to his waistcoat pocket, exactly like Lord Bunting's in the portrait.

"I'm sure your pocket watch will tell me the time as well as any wristwatch," I simpered.

The expression on his face as he glanced down at my fingertip was pure horror. When I gave another little tug, his brow furrowed.

"Oh, for heaven's sake, whaddya know?" He clapped his hand to his watch pocket. "I must have forgotten to set my granddaddy's watch on its chain this morning. Do you know, I've had a weird feeling all day that there was something I'd forgotten in my dressing room this morning."

Miss Harnett's dressing room, I wanted to say.

"No, wait, I can picture it now. It's lying sure as a statue on my writing desk in my study."

The Bursar's study.

Withdrawing my hand, I smiled coquettishly at his feeble excuses. I was sure now his pocket watch did not exist. It was as fake a prop as his fancy pen and car. That gave me the courage to sustain my controlling tone.

"Well, be quick about it if you want my help. I can't be late for my next class."

He dusted down his waistcoat with both hands as if to remove all trace of my touch.

"It's your darned girls again, Miss Lamb. I don't know what they have against me, but they've pulled a second stunt on me."

Actually, their third attempted prank. I wondered whether Miss Harnett had punished the gunpowder plotters yet.

"What have they done this time?"

"Something quite disgusting. I want them punished."

He grabbed my arm abruptly as if to steer me somewhere, and I shook him off immediately.

"I'm sorry, Miss Lump, I'm forgetting my manners. Please come with me to the forecourt to see the evidence. I hope you have a strong stomach, especially so soon after lunch."

More intrigued than I cared to admit, I accompanied Earl down the corridor, past the marble stairs, through the great oak front door and on to the forecourt. Since moving into Miss Harnett's suite, he'd taken to parking his white Rolls-Royce directly under the staffroom window, an unmissable reminder to us teachers of his supposedly superior status.

He led me round to the front of his car and pointed accusingly, his eyes averted.

"There! You see? Right there on the bonnet! What did I tell you? Those children of yours are monsters!"

Clear as day on the gleaming white paintwork, the remains of a neatly dissected bird lay in a pink splodge of fresh blood: the beak and claws and a small purplish organ which I guessed from its shape to be the liver.

"What perverted child among your little darlings would do that to the car of an esteemed visitor?"

His pointing finger was shaking with rage.

Something warm and soft brushed the backs of my calves, accompanied by a low engine-like hum.

"Why, hello, McPhee. You have been busy!"

I bent down to stroke the top of the cat's head, and she nuzzled my hand in fellowship. I didn't usually attempt to pick McPhee up, but I wanted to make it very clear to Earl whose side I was on. I scooped the cat up into my arms and smiled, feeling like Blofeld, the James Bond villain, except McPhee was black instead of white.

"I think we've found your culprit, Earl." I tried not to smile too broadly. "The only thing McPhee is guilty of is being a cat."

I held one of McPhee's front paws and made it point to the bird's remains on the car bonnet.

"It's what cats do. If I were you, I'd be flattered that McPhee had brought me a gift. Do you still want the culprit punished? Should I put her in detention? Make her write lines? Send her to bed without supper? Whichever you pick, it won't change her nature. She's just what she appears to be on the outside. I find that quite refreshing."

I hardly recognised this new assertive me, but I was enjoying myself.

McPhee was starting to wriggle, so I set her gently on the ground, where without a trace of remorse, she sat back and started to wash her left hind leg.

To give Earl a fair chance to reply, I fell silent, but he just gawped in turn at the cat and his car bonnet, or hood, as he had forgotten to call it.

"Come on, McPhee." I turned on my heel and clicked my fingers above the cat's nose to attract her attention. "I think it's time we got on with our day."

As I strutted back to the front door, McPhee marching by my side with military precision, my shoulders were shaking with silent laughter.

30

Tunnel of Love

"Hot tip, folks, if you're thinking of asking the Bursar for money for your department, don't do it today."

Joe made his announcement to a packed staffroom just before Miss Harnett was due to arrive for the morning's staff briefing.

"In fact, you might like to leave it for about three years."

Felicity Button gasped.

"I hope he doesn't plan to cut my budget for cookery ingredients, or we'll have no food to sell at the Christmas Fair. You can't make an omelette without any eggs."

Mavis sank down into her usual armchair with a thud. "But I'm desperate for some new Ordnance Survey maps. The ones I'm using to teach Year 9 orienteering are more sticky tape than map."

Oriana frowned.

"If I can't get some new calculators for Year 8 soon, they'll have to do all their sums in their heads. It'll add hours to their prep."

"First world problem," murmured Mavis. She always thought her subject was the centre of the world, which for a geography teacher is fair enough. We each thought our own department the most important.

"Has something upset the Bursar, Joe?" I asked, passing by his armchair on the way to my usual perch on the window seat.

"Not something, but someone. No prizes for guessing who that someone might be."

"Oh no, what has Earl been up to now?" asked Nicolette. "I thought the Bursar was preoccupied with helping Miss Harnett move all her stuff into Honeysuckle yesterday."

After a couple of weeks of trying to live in the disused dormitory, Miss Harnett had finally succumbed to his offer of Honeysuckle Lodge.

"Cohabiting with the Bursar?" queried Mavis. "Isn't that against school rules? We're not allowed to have so much as a cup of tea in a colleague's flat."

Felicity began offering round a tin of home-made shortbread fingers.

"She told me she was only taking the Bursar's house on condition that he stayed in the butler's flat. These are too misshapen to sell at the Christmas Fair, by the way. Oh, and Judith, twelve."

I was careful to take just the one biscuit this time.

The room fell silent as the door swung open to admit Miss Harnett for our daily pre-school pep talk.

* * *

"I don't know about the Bursar, but Hairnet seems less than happy," I said to Joe as we were leaving the staffroom after the briefing. "You'd think she'd be glad to get her privacy back, even though she doesn't like being at a distance from the girls."

Joe appraised me from the corner of his eye.

"You still haven't twigged, have you?"

"Twigged what?"

We paused at the entrance hall to part company, he to head to the pavilion, me to the classroom courtyard.

"Hairnet's other secret. Meet me in your classroom after lunch, where we won't have anyone listening in, and I'll tell you what it is."

I was less than attentive to the girls' conversation at my lunch table that day, racking my brains as to what Miss Harnett's big secret might be.

When Joe rapped on my classroom door, I was glad to close the exercise book I'd been staring at for the last five minutes. I must have read the essay title ten times, but if Joe had asked me what it was, I couldn't have told him.

I called to Joe to come in and he stopped at the doormat to remove his muddy trainers before loping over to sit on the pupil's desk nearest my own. His loose turquoise tracksuit trousers rustled as he made himself comfortable.

"Not interrupting, I hope, Miss Lamb?"

"Please do."

I pushed the pile of exercise books away from me.

"So, what's this big secret that's not safe to tell me in the staffroom?"

"Honestly, Gemma, I'm surprised you've not yet guessed. You're usually pretty astute."

I laid down my red pen.

"Well, go on, then, put me out of my misery. Or at least give me a clue."

A slow smile spread over his face.

"OK, a clue. You of all people, after the shenanigans in the mausoleum before half term, ought to be aware of Lord Bunting's tunnels."

I pursed my lips.

"Of course I know about Lord Bunting's tunnels. Everyone knows about the tunnels, even the greenest Year 7."

"But do you know where they all are? If I asked you to draw a map of them, what would it look like?"

Feeling as if I was in a Geography lesson being put on the spot by Miss Brook, I seized the whiteboard marker and turned my back on Joe to sketch a rough outline of the school. I included the boundary walls, the main house, the lodges, the mausoleum, and the walled garden. Then I put a cross in the middle of the walled garden.

"That's the entrance to the first one I found out about, because that's where you introduced me back in September to Max Security, when he popped up out of the ground like a meerkat in battledress. Do you remember? It was when you took me on the staff tour of the estate."

I added another cross in the middle of the mausoleum.

"And there's another hatch here, concealed by a cupboard, from which a tunnel leads to the garden of Rose Lodge."

I marked another cross on Max's lawn, and hesitated before adding a fourth at the cattle grid halfway down the drive.

"I think there's one here, from which Max likes to observe visiting vehicles at the beginning and end of term. I'm guessing maybe one by the pavilion? Is it old enough or was it built after Lord Bunting had died?"

When Joe nodded, I quickly sketched in his hut and added another x. After that I could only guess.

"The swimming pool isn't from Lord Bunting's time, so I'm disregarding that. But if I were Lord Bunting, I'd have wanted one to go to my private suite, so I could have the fun of using the network for my own purposes. It would be a great way to get from one part of my estate to another in bad weather without getting cold or wet."

"Spot on."

I added another x roughly where Miss Harnett's study would be.

"And where might you want that tunnel to go to?"

I considered.

"To all of those places marked x, I suppose. I'd want my suite to be the hub of my network. With the possible exception of the mausoleum. I don't think I'd want to visit my own grave before I died. Besides, I know the mausoleum one goes only to Max's garden."

"That's where you're wrong. There's a second hatch in the mausoleum, quite separate from the one you saw before half term, and they're not connected to each other.

211

The other one is behind the empty plinth. Each leads to a different tunnel."

Joe got up from the desk to join me by the whiteboard, gently taking the marker pen from my hand to add a second cross in the mausoleum. Then, starting at the Headmistress's suite, he drew a starburst of lines, going to almost all of the crosses on the map. He added another cross to the grotto beside the lake, then a line from there to Miss Harnett's suite. I had no idea there was a hatch in the grotto, despite passing it many times. The lake was one of my favourite destinations when I wanted a bit of fresh air. Finally, Joe joined the cross in the Headmistress's suite to the one at the cattle grid, then continued it right up to the back garden of the Bursar's lodge – or rather, the Headmistress's lodge now.

I put my hand over my mouth.

"You mean there's a secret passage between the Headmistress's suite and Honeysuckle Lodge?"

"And between her suite and the mausoleum."

I nodded. "I can see why she'd get a lot of use from the one to the mausoleum, seeing how much time she spends there."

"But whenever I've seen her there, she's only ever left via the main door, same as everyone else. I thought it was the only way out until I discovered the hatch in the cupboard."

Joe began idly to fill in details of the school's sports facilities on my map – the golf course, the tennis courts, the pitches.

"Well, of course. She's not daft. She doesn't want to give the game away. Can you imagine the pranks the girls would get up to if they knew how to access the tunnel network? As it was for Lord Bunting, one of the chief benefits for Hairnet is that she can traverse the estate, whatever the weather, without getting buttonholed by pupils or staff. It's like having her own private transport system."

"Or a cloak of invisibility. Just like the Medicis in medieval Florence. Well, not literally. I went there once on an A Level Art trip. The Medicis had the equivalent of Bunting's tunnel network, except it was overhead. They called it the Vasari corridor. It connected the Palazzo Vecchio to the Pitti Palace, where the Duke lived, via the Uffizi Gallery, the Ponte Vecchio and the Boboli Gardens. They must have had a wonderful view of the city from above, all the beautiful sights without the smells and the noise."

Joe grinned.

"That's one thing Lord Bunting's system doesn't offer: a good view." He handed the marker pen back to me.

"Now I think about it, I've seen Hairnet by the lake a couple of times this term and wondered how she managed to get back to school without me spotting her on the way."

"She likes to nip out to the walled garden to pick her own flowers, too."

"But the cattle grid? Why does that appeal to her?"

Joe laughed. "I confess I've never seen her there. Nor at my pavilion. She's not as sporting as Lord Bunting was. Which leaves…"

I stared at the map, then I gasped.

"Oh, my word! Honeysuckle Lodge!"

Joe's eyes were twinkling with mischief.

"It runs from bedroom to bedroom, apparently. From Hairnet's bedroom to the Bursar's. Remember, the lodges are single-storey, so the bedrooms are on the ground floor."

I seized the board eraser and immediately started to destroy the evidence.

"Oi! What about my lovely drawing of my sports empire?" Joe reached out to grab the eraser from me, but I snatched it quickly away, holding it behind my back with both hands, laughing.

"My whiteboard, my rules!"

I ran down the aisle passage between the desks, holding the eraser playfully above my head.

"To me, to me!" he cried, standing with his back to the board, feet planted firmly apart, spreading his arms out wide like a goal shoot in netball. My heart was racing at this unexpected bit of fun, and I stopped to catch my breath. Then I caught sight of the clock on the wall.

"No, seriously, Joe," I began to walk back towards him, "we must rub it all out before the girls get here. We don't want to spoil Miss Harnett's privacy, nor the Bursar's, by allowing them to see it."

We both started at the sound of a distinctive cough outside in the courtyard.

"Nor must we let on to Earl Bunting," said Joe.

I turned round just in time to see Earl's head of shiny dark hair bob past my classroom window in the direction of the main school building. Then I ran to the board to wipe off every spot of ink.

31

Tunnel Vision

So the Bursar's passion for Miss Harnett was reciprocal, their secret liaison unobserved as they scurried like rabbits between his burrow and hers.

I struggled to take the news in.

"But she's always so dismissive of him in public."

Joe settled down again on the desk.

"Of course she is. That's part of the camouflage for the sake of the girls and their parents. Just as I'm always telling them what a rotten English teacher you are."

I lobbed the board eraser at his head, but he caught it with a cry of "Owzat!"

"Mind you, Oriana's put-downs are genuine," he continued. "I don't know why she can't just let her mother be happy, after her biological father treated her so badly."

"Misplaced loyalty? All the same, poor Bursar. No wonder he was so cross about being banished to the attic, away from the arms of his beloved."

Joe broke into a smile at my purple prose.

"Spot the English teacher!"

I reined myself back in.

"To know Hairnet is sleeping in his actual bed while he's holed up in the butler's flat is just adding insult to injury."

"I wouldn't go feeling too sorry for them. I mean, nobody's made them be this secretive. He could have made an honest woman of Hairnet years ago if he'd a mind to. Or vice versa."

"Hairnet doesn't need the Bursar to prove she's honest. I've never met a woman with greater integrity."

"You're right, Gemma. But hey, as a commitment-phobe, you would take her side, wouldn't you?"

I would have chucked my board eraser at his head again if he hadn't still been clutching it. Then at my next thought, my irritation evaporated.

"Hang on, if the Bursar and Hairnet can hook up in the tunnels, surely Lord Bunting could have pursued a secret liaison with a woman living in Honeysuckle Lodge?"

Joe passed me the eraser.

"Presumably Lord Bunting originally built the tunnel from the lodge to show off the fruits of his invention to visitors as soon as they arrived at the entrance to the estate. But after his vow of celibacy, he could have fathered any number of illegitimate children in Honeysuckle Lodge undetected. The tunnels would have allowed him to do so while preserving his own reputation and Lady Bunting's dignity. I wonder whether any single women lived in Honeysuckle Lodge in those days? Before modern contraception, an illicit liaison with a woman under a certain age would be almost bound to produce offspring."

"You mean Earl Bunting's great-whatever grandmother who fled to the States? Mary O'Flaherty?"

I flipped my diary open at the school timetable.

"As soon as I can catch Judith Gosling, I'll ask her to search the family archive to see who was in residence at Honeysuckle Lodge at the time Earl claims his ancestor emigrated to America."

Joe chewed on a fingernail in thought.

"You do realise, Gemma, that you're on a trajectory to prove Earl Bunting's claim to the estate? Aren't we meant to be doing the opposite?"

I looked at him levelly.

"Like Miss Harnett, I'm nothing if not honest. No matter what I think of Earl Bunting as a person, it's in the school's long-term interest if we find out the truth."

32

On the Run

Before I had the chance to quiz Judith about Honeysuckle Lodge's former occupants, Max opened up another direction of enquiry. Diligent internet searching beyond the West Bradford Wedding Cars website had revealed the name of the proprietor, and a description that showed it could not possibly have been Earl. He read aloud a news report he'd found in the archive of the *Bradford Telegraph and Argus*.

"Leslie Dent, 54, corpulent and florid, struggled for breath as he blamed the illegal activities of his company on an alleged third party, of whose existence he has been unable to produce evidence. He claimed the fraudulent insurance and MOT certificates for his fleet of top-of-the-range wedding hire vehicles, all prestigious brands, had been the work of a new partner who had seemed highly plausible until he'd reportedly absconded with the supposed premiums in one of said vehicles. In the absence of any evidence to confirm the existence of a third party, Dent was found guilty on a plethora of accounts, including operating vehicles without insurance or MOT and running a vehicle hire company under invalid licence plates. Most assets of West Bradford Wedding Cars have been seized by HMRC in lieu of overdue tax, and the remaining assets are being retained by liquidators under a bankruptcy order. Five of the luxury vehicles registered to the company have been impounded. The sixth is as yet unaccounted for."

I grimaced.

"I can't help feeling that with a name like Dent, the poor man might have been better off pursuing a career that didn't involve cars."

"Don't let yourself get distracted by sympathy for Dent." Max brandished his print-out of the article at me. "He may be making the whole thing up to try to save himself. He may be guilty as charged, and of much more besides. Even so, I think we have enough evidence to merit further investigations of our own."

I took the print-out from him to reread and laughed at the headline: "One Dent Too Many in Local Car Crime Con".

"So, while this proves Earl can't be the proprietor of the company, there are two explanations as to how he has come to be driving that fancy car. He might have bought or hired it from Dent in good faith before his arrest and be its legal owner. Or he might have been a co-conspirator with Dent, the alleged third party, and driven off in it. Earl could still be Lord Bunting's legal heir as well as being a fraudster. The two things aren't mutually exclusive."

Max tapped his nose knowingly.

"Or Dent may not be a co-conspirator at all, but a poor innocent outwitted by a duplicitous Earl Bunting."

"Even if Earl's the latter, he could still be rightful heir to St Bride's, but we can dob him up for fraud or deception." I was starting to speak like the girls. "If he is the missing third party, he'll almost certainly go to prison. But it would be a short-term solution at best."

"But Gemma, don't you see? If he's committed fraud once, at the expense of Leslie Dent, there's a strong chance he's doing it again now. Fraudsters are generally serial offenders. Once they pull off one scam, they carry on. The more they get away with, the more they're convinced that they're fireproof. Ultimately, they take a risk too far and get caught. Classic."

I turned the print-out over, hoping there might be more detail on the other side, but it was blank.

"I don't suppose you've found any descriptions of the alleged third party?"

Max shook his head.

"Nope, but I reckon there's a chance that it's Earl. With the details given here, I can find out where Dent's being held pending sentencing, and who his lawyer is. And I bet I can engineer a meeting with the lawyer if I offer the lure of a suspect to clear Dent's name."

I considered this.

"Why don't you just go to the police?"

Max shook his head.

"No can do, Gemma. Miss Harnett and the governors wouldn't take kindly to my dragging the cops into St Bride's. The girls' parents would have forty fits. Besides, it would undermine my authority as school security officer."

I could see a flaw in his theory.

"If Earl stole his Rolls-Royce from Dent's yard, how come it hasn't been traced? You'd think that traffic cameras would pick up any licence plate being sought by the police."

Max looked at me for a minute, deep in thought.

"There are ways and means, Gemma. I'm willing to bet that tucked away in the firm's garages somewhere is a machine for minting licence plates embossed with the company name. Which means it would be simple for anyone to produce any plates they wished, including fake registrations. I'm willing to bet that Earl cranked out his BLISS plate, knowing it was an unregistered number, fixed it to his car of choice and sneaked off in it before anyone noticed. Then he drove all the way here at well under the speed limit, but not so slowly as to draw attention to himself, all the while being careful to avoid getting stopped on the spot for minor traffic offences. No jumping the lights, no phone calls at the wheel, not even eating a sandwich along the way."

I was warming to his theory.

"And even if he did get caught on camera, how could the police possibly trace him? A fake registration would lead precisely nowhere on their database. Especially as Earl had covered up the company name with white paint."

A light appeared in Max's eye.

"Do you know what else I'd do to discourage anyone from stopping me along the way?"

I shrugged.

"I can't think of anything."

"I'd – no, hang on, Gemma, let me surprise you. Do you know where Earl is right now?"

"I just saw him heading for the pool. He'll be there for hours yet. He loves swimming, and the girls don't have any lessons there today, so he'll have the place to himself. Unlikely to emerge before suppertime, I'd say."

No wonder Earl's hair dye was fading.

I passed the cutting back to Max, who folded it as precisely as a piece of origami and returned it to one of his trouser pockets.

"Can you do me a favour, Gemma? It'll be dark by teatime. I assume you'll be in the staffroom then, so you can stand guard for me."

He must have noticed me flinch.

"Don't worry, nothing dangerous. All you need to do is sit in your usual spot on the window seat, which won't look suspicious at all. At the same time, keep a watch out of the window as I check what's in the boot of Earl's car. Try not to let anyone close the curtains. If they do, you'll just have to sneak behind them. Knock on the window to warn me if you see Earl coming. It'll only take me a minute to break into his car boot. Worst case scenario: he catches me in the act. Then I'll just say I saw someone tampering with his lock and came to check for damage."

I grinned.

"I wish I had your nerve, Max."

Max straightened his back as if on military parade.

"Years of training, Gemma. But what kind of training, I'm not at liberty to say."

"And I wouldn't dare ask, Max. Best of luck!"

223

33

Buttonholed

As it turned out, I didn't have to watch over the car at all, because Earl accosted me in the staffroom as soon as I entered at afternoon break. Shuffling sideways as he spoke to me, I managed to turn him round so that his back was to the window and I had a clear view of the forecourt. Max, heartened by the sight of Earl's back, stuck his thumb up to me to signal he was on the case.

Earl had driven his car forward into the parking space outside the staffroom, so the boot was at the far end, out of my sight. I'd have to wait till Max came round to the front to show me what he'd found. In the meantime, I needed to keep Earl talking as long as it took Max to do his stuff.

"Miss Lung, you seem to know a lot about cats," was Earl's opening gambit.

I wondered where this was leading.

"We had cats at home when I was growing up."

To my eternal regret, the last of my childhood cats had died of old age while I was still estranged from my parents.

"Good, then you can help me get rid of that black devil of Caroline's."

For a second, I wondered who Caroline was. No-one called the Headmistress by her first name in the staffroom.

"You mean McPhee?"

"Is that what she calls the little demon? Yes, if that's the same creature who desecrated my automobile the other day."

I struggled to keep a straight face.

"Why, has she left you another little offering on your car?" The moment I'd spoken, I realised that was a stupid thing to say. If he dashed over to the window to check, he'd catch Max red-handed, and it would all be my fault. "Or is there something else she's been up to?"

He folded his arms.

"No, but I know the wretched critter is plaguing my apartment. No matter how carefully I close all my doors and windows – and believe me, I'm keeping all my windows tight shut against your dreadful English weather – she finds her way in."

When I'd first come to live and work at the school, I'd been unnerved by McPhee's uncanny ability to walk through closed doors. Only after spending half term with my parents and their new cat Sparky had I remembered that all cats seem to have this quality, thanks to their silent tread. Cat burglars are so called for good reason.

"That's because you're on her territory, Earl. Just because Miss Harnett isn't there at the moment doesn't switch off McPhee's animal instincts. She still sees it as her

226

space." I wanted to clarify that I considered his occupation temporary. "Unless you want to go around marking it as your territory, there's nothing you can do about it."

I admit I wasn't trying very hard to solve his problem.

"Yes, there is." Dr Fleming brought her cup of tea over to join us. "You can get a bigger cat to pull rank. That's what my father does to keep neighbours' cats off his garden."

"What, you mean I've got to get a bigger cat to fend McPhee off?"

Dr Fleming flashed a reassuring smile.

"Oh no, not a whole cat. Just its dung. You see, my father lives near a zoo, so he fertilises his rose beds with lion manure. Now not another cat ventures near. Does the trick perfectly."

"You mean you recommend daubing my beautiful apartment with – ugh!"

Dr Fleming sneaked me a wink as Earl broke away and stormed out of the door.

I was so busy laughing, along with everyone else within earshot, that I almost forgot my mission. Then, after thanking Dr Fleming for coming to my rescue, I dashed over to the window to check on Max.

The car boot was wide open, and Max was just stepping to one side to give me a clear view of his trophy. Now he held it up for me to see: a life-size dummy of a bride in flowing white dress, face modestly concealed behind a matching lace veil. If strategically positioned in the back seat, it could easily convince passing traffic that it was the real thing.

But you never see a bride travelling unaccompanied. In the bridal car, she would always be with either her groom or whoever was to give her away. As if reading my mind (which I wouldn't put past Max), he returned to the boot to replace the bride, before reappearing with a slightly larger dummy of a grey-haired man in a morning suit, complete with floral buttonhole. Father of the bride.

I wondered whether Earl had thought to make his getaway trip from Bradford in a chauffeur's outfit, peaked cap masking his face from traffic cameras. No-one would dream of stopping a chauffeur-driven wedding car, complete with the bride and her father, especially when it was being driven according to the law. The car might get plenty of waves and honks for good luck from passing motorists, but only a heartless police officer would interfere with the happiest day of a bride's life.

Perhaps, in his arrogance, Earl had thought it was the happiest day of his too.

34

Off the Record

My first thought after Joe's latest revelation was to wonder whether Lord and Lady Bunting had shared a bedroom. I had a vague recollection that the Headmistress's study, with its delicate floral plaster ceiling and soft pink silk wallpaper, had once been Lady Bunting's room.

In the end, it was another question I needed to ask Judith Gosling.

"Yes, Hairnet's study was Lady Bunting's bedroom and Lord Bunting's was what is now Hairnet's sitting room. In Victorian times, it was the gentry's custom to have separate bedchambers for husband and wife. These would often be adjoining with an interconnecting door. I believe that still applies to the Queen and Prince Philip at Buckingham Palace."

"So, Lady Bunting would not have known what was going on in Lord Bunting's bedroom, if he kept quiet?"

"I suppose so. But if you're thinking he was carrying on an extra-marital affair while his wife slept just metres away, that doesn't seem very likely to me."

"How about if he could find a way of discreetly removing himself from his bedroom while she thought he was fast asleep?"

"You mean the tunnels? Yes, of course. They'd be ideal."

Her eyes flickered to and fro as if she was drawing a mental map of the tunnel network.

"The tunnel to Honeysuckle Lodge would be the most likely. I can't imagine him arranging a secret tryst in the mausoleum, having built it for his own tomb. The Victorians were much more open about death than we are. The poor souls had to be to cope with such a high rate of mortality. But I can't imagine any respectable woman agreeing to meet in a tomb for a romantic assignation."

I grinned. "There's a poem about that." I couldn't resist quoting from Andrew Marvell's *To His Coy Mistress*, which my Year 11 class was currently studying, amid much sniggering.

"The grave's a fine and private place,
But none, I think, do there embrace."

Judith smiled. "A liaison in a more romantic spot, by the lake or in the walled garden, would be too easily discovered by a house guest taking a late-night stroll, or by a gamekeeper. Not to mention chilly."

"Gamekeeper? I didn't know there were any game on the estate to keep."

"In those days, Lord Bunting raised pheasants for shooting parties, and there was a herd of deer in the woodland, plus the inevitable wild rabbits."

"How awful if in the moonlight, he or his lady friend were mistaken for wild game and shot."

Judith laughed. "Fair game, you might say. But by process of elimination, if he was going to sneak off anywhere, it would be either to the sports pavilion or to Honeysuckle Lodge."

My eyes widened at the thought of Joe's pavilion. Had Lord Bunting once sat in that old armchair of Joe's, his illicit lover on his lap?

"I know which I'd prefer," she added.

"Surely Honeysuckle Lodge would be occupied by a servant? Isn't that the point of the lodges? I thought they functioned a bit like tollbooths, with a minion manning the gates so that only authorised visitors may enter. I didn't think it would be home to the sort of woman who would have an affair with Lord Bunting?"

Judith passed a hand across her neat hair in thought.

"Yes, but that wouldn't have stopped him. Plenty of Victorian gentlemen took advantage of female servants. Why not Lord Bunting?"

She sounded disappointed in him. I wondered whether she was a little in love with Lord Bunting herself. There's a shortage of love interests when you work in a girls' boarding school.

"If he was carrying on with whichever female servant lived in Honeysuckle, that would account for why it has much better fixtures and fittings than Rose Lodge. I don't suppose you've ever been inside either of the lodges, Gemma?"

"No, of course not."

The rule against colleagues visiting each other's school accommodation had been a puzzle to me when I first joined, seeming an unreasonable constraint on our liberty. Now it was starting to make much more sense. Could it simply be a subterfuge to cover for Miss Harnett and the Bursar's affair and their secret liaisons at Honeysuckle Lodge?

Judith looked smug.

"Well, I've been to both. To Rose Lodge when my car broke down on the drive near the main gates. I was returning from my evening off late at night and knocked on Max's door to help me fix it. Another time I had to go to Honeysuckle on official business to deliver an urgent letter to the Bursar on his day off. Just a glimpse into Max's entrance hall was enough to show me that Rose Lodge is austere, almost clinical, with the feel of a Victorian hospital: dark parquet floor, dark green tiles halfway up the wall, cream walls above, plain steel lampshade on the single ceiling light. Probably suits him, with his militaristic ways. Whereas Honeysuckle is all gleaming brass fittings, Arts and Crafts carvings on the woodwork, William Morris wallpaper. It has the same innate luxury of St Bride's House, but in miniature, like a dolls' house, whereas Rose Lodge feels strictly below stairs."

No wonder the Bursar had been so miffed about moving to the butler's flat.

"Wow. Like a stately home but cheaper to heat and less dusting. So whichever servant lived there must have been a favourite."

A twinkle appeared in Judith's kindly eyes.

"Funnily enough, I don't know who lived in the lodges when Lord Bunting was in residence. I've never seen any official records in the archives of the family or the school, although I'm guessing there must have been a logbook of some kind."

My disappointment was short-lived.

"The school may not have a record, but I know someone who has at least a partial account: Earl."

Judith blinked.

"Earl? What's he doing with them? If he's been raiding my archive cupboard behind my back –"

I raised my hand to stop her.

"No, nothing like that. But he does have a new acquisition for your cupboard that I'm sure we'll both find fascinating."

"Lord Bunting's will? Yes, I know about that, Gemma. There's always been a copy in the archive cupboard. I remember the first time I read it, thinking it looked straightforward. Before I went into teaching, I was a paralegal, working for a law firm specialising in inheritance. Of course, at the time of Lord Bunting's death, no-one knew of any surviving children, so that part of the will would have been disregarded once they'd put the requisite advertisement in *The Times* for any heirs to come forward and received no response. There was also a lavish obituary in the papers. I confess I'd disregarded that

233

possibility too until Hairnet asked me to research any illegitimate line of descent."

"No, not the will," I said. "There was something else that Earl was going to show me not long after he'd arrived: his ancestor's journal, containing details of her affair with Lord Bunting and her emigration, with child. If she emigrated long before his death, no way would she have read about his will in *The Times*, nor his death notice."

Judith gasped.

"Earl offered to show you that and you turned it down?"

"Oh no, I didn't turn it down. We just got diverted and I'd forgotten about it. We had gone out to fetch it from his car when we discovered the girls had coated his car in mud."

Judith laughed.

"Oh yes, I remember. Best prank so far this term."

"Then of course I had to track down the girls and make them clean it, then there was the Guy Fawkes party that same night, and his journal went clean out of my head. He must still have it. I bet if you asked him nicely, he'd let you put it in the archives for safekeeping."

"It might make him feel more secure, as if he's been formally received into the Bunting dynasty. And it is true that it would be safer there than in his car or apartment. The library is ever under the watchful eye of Max's surveillance camera, much to Mavis's annoyance."

I tried not to think about the times I'd been alone or with Joe in the library, believing I was unobserved. Next time I saw Max, I would blush.

"With the added bonus for us –" I locked eyes with my co-conspirator "– that we could then read it at our leisure!"

35

Diary Dates

"Psst!"

A burst of wintry sunshine had lured me down to the lake after lunch. I really needed some fresh air, and time and space to think about recent developments. But as I walked past the grotto, a hissing sound from among the rocks alerted me to Max, emerging from the tunnel through a manhole in the ground.

As he closed the hatch behind him, I could see why I'd never spotted this particular tunnel entrance before. It was entirely covered by a fake rock, lightweight but realistic.

"Gemma, good news!"

Max beckoned me to join him in the little cave. Out of the sun, the temperature must have been at least ten degrees lower, and I shivered beneath my winter coat.

"What is it, Max? Have you managed to speak to Dent?"

He was looking very pleased with himself.

"Not quite, but I will soon. When I emailed his solicitor, he replied immediately. Took my bait straight away."

"So what happened next?"

I wrapped my arms about me for warmth.

"I gave him an outline of our suspicions, but not enough to answer any of his questions categorically. For that, I requested a meeting. Long story short: he's agreed to see me, and if my evidence justifies it, he'll arrange for me to visit Dent in custody to answer a few questions of our own. I'm seeing him on Thursday."

"In the middle of the week in term-time? Will Hairnet let you leave the premises?"

Max beamed.

"No, of course not. The girls' security must come first, as ever. But the solicitor, Anthony Fullerton, is so excited about our evidence that he's agreed to visit me in my lodge at lunchtime. I'm not usually patrolling then, as the girls and staff are all safely ensconced in the Trough, so I've put an hour of my time at his disposal. Wish me luck, Gemma."

He lifted the hatch and stepped down on to the first rung of the metal ladder leading to the tunnel below. I gave him a double thumbs-up of approval.

"Over the top! Or rather, underneath it!"

As I stepped out of the grotto back into the daylight, a shaft of December sunshine felt unexpectedly warm on my face.

* * *

Any feelings of contentment evaporated as I rounded the far end of the lake to find Earl sitting on an old wrought iron bench. His arms were spread proprietorially along the back and his legs, crossed at the ankles, stretched out at full length in front of him. He was greedy for space. Although of lean build, he'd managed to fill four seats all by himself. With thick hedges behind the seat, I had no option but to walk in front of him, other than to turn round and retrace my steps. But I wasn't going to allow Earl to feel he'd won.

He saw my approach but did not budge. After glancing behind me to check no-one else was in earshot, I decided to take the plunge – not into the lake, but into challenging Earl about his ancestor's journal. I summoned up all my dramatic abilities, taking my inspiration from young Abigail.

"Earl, how nice to see you."

I half expected him to fall about laughing at this false sentiment, but his inflated ego allowed him to believe my pleasure was genuine. To my surprise, he lowered his arms to his sides, uncrossed his ankles, and moved along the bench so I could sit beside him. At any other time, I'd have declined his invitation, but now it played into my hands.

I tried to put him off his guard.

"This is a lovely spot, isn't it?"

"Indeed it is, Miss Lame. Chilly after the climate I'm used to, of course, but I must say I'm enjoying getting to know every corner of my property at last."

Earl clasped his hands over his stomach like someone who has just enjoyed a feast.

That led nicely into my mission.

"Absolutely, Earl. It's not just for yourself that you're staking your claim. You're part of a long tradition. You must update the archives for posterity."

A flicker of doubt crossed his face as he turned to look at me.

"I thought I'd done that already. You saw me write on that poster."

I cringed on Judith's behalf at his description of her painstaking piece of calligraphy.

"I didn't just mean adding your name to the family tree." I waved a hand dismissively. "For the sake of posterity, you should add anything you can to the family archive in the library."

He perked up.

"You mean for future generations?"

I cringed again, this time at the thought of a bevy of young Earl lookalikes cavorting across the lawns, but persevered.

"Yes, yes, of course. For your descendants."

"Hmm, I suppose I should."

He gazed dreamily at the weeping willow on the far side of the lake, its long fronds trailing in the dark water.

"I guess it'll make quite a story, huh? I'm picturing my grandson all grown up, telling his new wife on her first tour of the estate that she has his dear granddaddy to thank for her good fortune. He'll tell her how I boldly reclaimed St Bride's for its rightful owners."

He really was a fantasist.

"I suppose most of your personal papers are tied up in the shipment coming over from the States, along with your other cars?"

His fabled baggage still hadn't arrived. Mavis had set up a sweepstake in the staffroom as to how long it would be before he announced that the ship bringing his things had unaccountably sunk, taking all his possessions with it. Joe reckoned there would be pirates involved, but we had just watched *Pirates of the Caribbean* together.

"In the meantime –" my heart beat faster as I cued up my shot "– you might like to start by depositing your ancestor's journal in the archive. The one you were going to show me a few weeks ago. We never got round to it, did we?" I crossed my fingers that he wouldn't remember why. "The Bursar told me the governors were most impressed by it."

"Well, of course they were. It includes indisputable evidence of my descent, but it's also where I keep my copies of the various birth certificates that trace the line of descent down to me."

This was good news.

"Then you must deposit it in the library for safekeeping. The library is the most secure room in the school."

"You mean because of that old witch, the librarian?"

"Mavis Brook is not a witch, she's a very kind lady. Don't let her gruff demeanour fool you. I'm talking about Max's surveillance cameras. Due to the value of the rare books in the library, he keeps every inch of space under scrutiny at all times."

This was an exaggeration on both counts. Most of the valuable books had long since been sold off to boost school funds, and there was only one camera in there. Max had better things to do than keep watch over the library.

Earl's ears pricked up.

"The books in there are valuable? They don't look that special to me."

I steered him back on track.

"So, if you'd care to pass your journal to Judith Gosling, who as Head of History manages the archive cupboard…"

He jumped to his feet.

"Why, thank you, Miss Lake. I'll do that straight away."

He touched a forefinger to his temple in an old-fashioned salute of gratitude.

This time my smile was genuine.

"The pleasure's all mine, Earl."

I just hoped Judith Gosling might find some flaws in his evidence that the governors had missed.

36

The Icing on the Gingerbread

"Anyone for gingerbread freaks? They taste better than they look."

Felicity's usual pride in her pupils' baking must have been a little dented by the bizarre appearance of today's offering to the staffroom: a tray of gingerbread men made with too runny a mixture. The carefully stamped forms had spread out on baking, blending in with each other. She'd given up trying to restore them to their intended human form and had just cut the big brown biscuit sheet into squares, each dotted at random with what had once been sultana buttons and raisin eyes, noses and mouths.

Judith and Joe jostled for first pick.

"Ooh, I love gingerbread," Judith enthused. "I don't care what shape it comes in."

I went to join her, avoiding the squares with startled expressions.

"Look on the bright side, Felicity. It feels less cruel than eating people-shaped ones."

Felicity rolled her eyes.

"Tell me about it. I've already had two girls trying to tell me they can't eat gingerbread men because they're vegetarian. They said they never eat anything with a face."

Earl wandered into the staffroom, following the scent of warm biscuits. But for a change, he hadn't just come to freeload. His prime aim was to buttonhole Judith. His precious journal tucked under his arm, he barged in between his quarry and Felicity.

"I've purposely cut out a couple for you that don't include the dried fruit," Felicity was saying to Judith, "so they'll have fewer carbs."

"Thanks, Felicity. Dried fruit is a bit of a nightmare for me. You wouldn't think something so shrivelled could contain so much sugar."

Earl snorted.

"On a diet, Miss Goshawk? That's not setting a very good example for the girls."

I was about to defend her when she turned on Earl herself, sufficiently affronted to make a rare public mention of her condition.

"No, Earl, I'm diabetic. I just need to know the carb content of anything I eat so I can give myself the right amount of insulin my body needs to process it. As one of your precious Bunting ancestors died of diabetes in the days before it could be treated, you ought to be a little more sympathetic."

Earl quickly backpedalled.

"My apologies. Yes, my ancestor. Diabetes runs in the Bunting family, of course. I have it too, you know. A fearful allergy. Pesky genes, eh?"

Before Judith could put him straight, he had the wit to produce his journal.

"For your archives, Miss Gander."

He held it out in both hands, clicked his heels and gave a little bow.

Immediately, Judith changed tack.

"Oh. Oh, I see. Thank you, Earl." She wiped her hands on her skirt to brush off any gingerbread crumbs. "I'll put it safely away in the family section of the archive cupboard straight after break."

Felicity, ever the peacemaker, offered Earl the tray of gingerbread. He took a step back as if it were poison.

"Not for me, thank you, Miss Zipper. Pesky diabetes, huh, Miss Gander?"

Tutting loudly, he left the staffroom.

There was silence, no-one knowing quite what to say. Then Judith, overcome with embarrassment at her outburst, raised the journal above her head for all to see.

"I'd better go and put this in the archive cupboard. But not without a thorough read first."

"Don't forget to tell us what you find, Judith!" called Mavis. "I'm hoping it proves Earl's a charlatan and we can boot him out without more ado."

"Fingers crossed," said Judith.

She opened the journal and started reading as she left the staffroom.

Dr Fleming stepped up to the gingerbread.

"What an ignoramus that man is," she said evenly. "Any fool knows diabetes is not an allergy, and it's not necessarily inherited."

"Talking out of his archive, as usual," said Joe, making us all laugh and returning the staffroom atmosphere to normal.

Mavis heaved herself up out of her armchair.

"All the more gingerbread for us."

After helping herself to the largest piece on the tray, she stooped to pick up a folded scrap of paper on the floor by my feet.

"Is this yours, Gemma?"

During the previous lesson, I'd written a note to myself – the phone number of Hector's House – to call about a book order, and put it in my pocket, intending to use the staffroom phone at break. But now the bell was ringing to summon the girls to their next lesson. I took the note from her, stuffing it back in my pocket to call at lunchtime instead.

"Thanks, Mavis."

When Felicity set the remains of the gingerbread on the coffee table for later, Mavis took two more large squares and put them in her pigeonhole.

37

Classroom Conflab

"Form an orderly queue, folks," Judith called from her desk without looking up. As I arrived in her classroom, she was still engrossed in Mary O'Flaherty's journal.

Judith's classroom was the neatest in the school, with desks in perfect rows, shelves of reference books lined up in date order, and posters pinned to the walls with more than the statutory drawing pin at each corner.

Although there was no school rule preventing us from visiting each other's classrooms, the staffroom was where we generally caught up with each other. Now, however, we'd nearly all devised a pretext to drop into Judith's classroom as soon as lunch was over.

"I think this is yours, Judith," said Dr Fleming, waving a shiny black hole punch.

The fuzzy grey blob in Mavis's upturned palm looked less appealing.

"Remember I borrowed some Blu-tack from you last term? I've come to return it."

"I've been meaning to read this book for ages," said Joe, grabbing the first volume that came to hand, the story of the Bayeux Tapestry.

Judith, reaching the last page of the journal, snapped the book shut. As we stood obediently in line, she looked up, lips pursed, brow creased in puzzlement.

"The plot thickens," she said slowly.

"So, what's your verdict, Judith?" I asked from my place halfway down the line. "Does the journal disprove Earl's claim?"

Judith looked up and down the queue to ensure she had our full attention before she spoke.

"Not as such."

Her intent audience gave a collective sigh of disappointment.

"But it does reveal some interesting and pertinent details."

A collective sharp intake of breath.

Everyone in the queue leaned sideways to get a better view. From where Judith was sitting, we must have looked like a Busby Berkeley dance troupe on an off day.

"Go on, then, sit down, everyone, and I'll tell you the gist of what I've discovered. Let's hope no girls call at the staffroom in the meantime as it looks like all the teachers are over here."

Just then the Bursar rapped on the door and marched in without waiting to be invited.

"Judith, I wanted to talk to you about your new textbook order," he was saying, waving a requisition sheet. "Good heavens, what's this, a mutiny?"

"Take a seat, Bursar, you're just in time," said Judith, seeing straight through his subterfuge. "I think it's important you hear this too. I know you can't tell us what went on at the governors' meeting when they accepted Earl Bunting's claim to the estate, but feel free to make any helpful indications if I'm on the right track. A cough or sneeze will do nicely."

The Bursar chose the seat in the back corner of the room, perhaps so he could gauge our reactions before sharing his.

Once we'd all settled down, Judith gave a small smile. She was enjoying herself.

"Here we go, then. I've skim-read the journal and certain things are clear. First point: this appears to be an authentic journal handwritten with a dip pen. The script is darker whenever the writer has just dipped her pen in the ink pot. The paper of the notebook looks, to my amateur eye, old enough to be Victorian. Mavis, as school librarian, you're the most familiar with books from Lord Bunting's era. Care to share your opinion?"

Mavis went to Judith's desk to examine the evidence, turning the fragile pages with reverence.

"I'd go a step further, Judith. In the school library, there used to be a few notebooks of the same vintage, from the same manufacturer, containing Bunting's engineering design notes and sketches."

Judith's jaw dropped.

"Really? I've never seen those in the archive. They sound fascinating. They'd be valuable too. Where are they?"

Mavis, hands on hips, turned to face the Bursar.

"Care to field that question, Bursar?"

The Bursar lowered his eyes, running a fingernail down a fault line in the desktop in front of him.

"I may have placed them with the Science Museum for safekeeping."

"Sold, more like," muttered Oriana.

Judith wanted to press on with her story.

"That's neither here nor there for our current purposes."

The Bursar let out a sigh of relief.

"Back to the journal, I'm pleased to say that it looks like an authentic Victorian record."

Mavis sat down again and shifted impatiently in her chair.

"We've ascertained that, Judith, so what does it actually say?"

Judith paused, choosing her words carefully to present the detached viewpoint of a historian.

"The journal is the personal and secret record of Mary O'Flaherty, a single woman in her early twenties. An Irish immigrant, she entered the Bunting household at the age of nineteen as a kitchen maid and progressed surprisingly quickly to the role of cook. This was a prestigious and responsible role in such an estate, normally held by a much older and more experienced woman. With it came the entitlement to live in Honeysuckle Lodge."

Felicity raised her hand.

"Rather a long way from her kitchens, Judith. The drive is nearly a mile long. If I'd been her and had to cook everyone's breakfasts, I'd have preferred to stay in St Bride's House."

"Indeed. In the very first entry, she remarks upon the fact that her new abode will add nearly an hour to her working day. But she alludes coyly to other benefits justifying her move."

Joe grimaced.

"Cooks with benefits, eh? I think we can guess what those are. Do they involve a certain tall, dark, handsome gentleman?"

Judith pursed her lips.

"She was a beautiful woman who early on in her employment caught the eye of her master. It seems her affair with Lord Bunting had long been mooted, his last child with Lady Bunting having died two years previously. She had to wait for Honeysuckle Lodge to become free when the previous cook, one Matilda Thompson, moved back to Yorkshire to live with her parents. Mary O'Flaherty's journal, only slightly encrypted for confidentiality, makes it clear that his surreptitious visits began the day after she had moved in, and ended only when she found herself with child."

"Poor Lady Bunting," I murmured.

"Don't worry, Gemma, according to Mary's journal, not a soul but Lord Bunting was party to the secret. And he did the decent thing, relatively speaking."

"What was that?" asked Dr Fleming. "Surely he was never going to leave his wife for a servant?"

"Of course not. Mary knew that. However, he promised at the start of their affair that should certain circumstances arise such that she could no longer fulfil the role of cook, he would guarantee her financial security and settle on her a generous annuity. She need never work again. In addition, she would receive a lump sum to enable her to buy a modest home and live rent free for life. He would also pay her passage to anywhere in the world where she might want to start a new life. All this was on condition that she never revealed him to be her child's father and that she and her child never set foot on the estate during his lifetime."

"Not a bad offer." Mavis sounded almost envious. She yearned for such security for her retirement, having lost her pension rights from her previous job.

Oriana sighed.

"It must have been tough on Lord Bunting, never to see their baby, not even knowing what it looked like, especially if Mary was as good looking as he was."

"Bit shallow, Miss Bliss," returned Mavis.

"Oh, she was beautiful all right," said Judith. "With sparkling blue eyes and glorious auburn curls."

Joe snorted in disdain.

"Conceited, too, if she wrote that in her journal."

"Oh, but she didn't." Judith opened the journal at a page she'd bookmarked and held it up to show us all. "You see, she's stuck in a love letter from Lord Bunting which addresses her attractions in some detail. Which, by the way, is further evidence of the journal's authenticity. The letter is recognisably in his hand."

I glanced at the wall clock. It was nearly time for afternoon school to begin.

"So, what you're saying, Judith, is that Earl's journal proves the theory you and I were discussing earlier that his ancestor was a servant put in the family way by Lord Bunting and paid to emigrate. So all Earl needs to do to prove his rights to St Bride's is demonstrate that he's descended from Mary O'Flaherty."

The Bursar interrupted. "Which he did. He showed the governors all the birth, death and marriage certificates linking him to her. They all agreed that Earl is indisputably Lord Bunting's natural descendant."

Mavis brushed his evidence aside.

"Anybody could buy those documents online, Bursar. I could order Lady Bunting's birth certificate, but it wouldn't mean I was her. Nor would it mean I owned St Bride's, more's the pity."

Judith nodded. "I'm afraid the worst is yet to come. In rather gloating terms, Mary also describes persuading Lord Bunting to remember her unborn child in his will, should his marriage have no natural progeny. Lord Bunting agreed. In those days, illegitimate children had no automatic rights of inheritance, so the inclusion of all issue would have to be specified in the will to be valid."

Felicity, who taught the girls the principles of will-making as part of her Essential Life Skills programme, immediately saw a flaw in the deal.

"But wouldn't such a will reveal his affair to Lady Bunting?"

"It may well be that Lady Bunting never saw the will," said Judith. "In those days women weren't involved in

253

business and legal matters. She would just trust her husband to make appropriate provision for her if she outlived him Which to be fair is what he did. He left her the estate in trust plus a generous allowance for as long as she remained in residence. If she remarried and moved away, her new husband would assume responsibility for her welfare, and she would forfeit the estate but not the personal allowance. After that, in the absence of a claim from his own issue, legitimate or otherwise, the estate was to be transformed into a boarding school for girls."

"How did Lady Bunting feel about that?" I wondered aloud.

"Entirely comfortable, it seems. In her journal, not long after she decided to have no more children, Lady Bunting writes that she is planning to put the idea of a girls' school to her husband. The idea was hers all along. She even suggests that this might be done in her lifetime, should she choose not to remarry. She considered remaining in residence as the school's founding headmistress. At last she would have dozens of children about her – the children she never had herself."

"Perhaps it was also her idea that preference should be given to motherless girls," put in Felicity. "That way she might see herself as their second mother."

There were a few moments' silence while we digested this poignant detail. Then Judith continued.

"Her husband worded his will carefully so that should she have sight of it after his death, she would not be hurt. He doesn't name names, he just states that his ultimate beneficiary will be his eldest surviving son or that son's eldest surviving son, and so on down the generations."

"Clever, or just superstitious?" asked Mavis. "He might have thought adding the names of his legitimate children by Lady Bunting would jinx their survival."

Felicity tapped her desk for emphasis.

"Clever in terms of saving on legal fees, at least, because it would spare him the expense of drawing up a new will every time one of his children died."

Judith nodded.

"Also clever because if he showed Mary the will, it would satisfy her that her child, if male, stood to inherit the estate, as promised."

We sat in silence, digesting Judith's insights and their implications for Earl's claim. Then Mavis thumped her desk.

"But it makes no sense. If Mary was assured that her child would inherit, why didn't she send him back to stake his claim? We know she and the kid weren't allowed to return to St Bride's, but only while Lord Bunting was still alive. Even if she'd set up home in the US, the price of the passage home for them both would be well worth the investment. Where was it she went again? Kentucky? Missouri? Earl said one of the southern states."

Judith laid a protective hand on the journal's frail cover. What a journey that book had taken, now going full circle back to where its life had begun.

"Actually, not the southern USA at all, but southern Ireland. Galway, to be precise. Mary O'Flaherty was the perfect picture of an Irish beauty, as Lord Bunting's love letter describes, from her flaming auburn curls to the tip of her nimble dancing feet. Yes, my friends, Lord Bunting's Irish mistress was a redhead, just like Earl."

38

Irish Fling

"The journal's dates tally with the old staff records in the butler's flat," added the Bursar. "I found the register of the servants' quarters in a tin box under the bed the other day. Goodness knows how long they've been there. They should have been in the archive cupboard."

"But what about the American connection?" asked Felicity. "Why does Earl claim to be from the States?"

"He may well be," replied the Bursar. "Plenty of Irish have emigrated to the States, from Victorian times up to the present day, so maybe at some point Mary's descendants did too. Have any of you ever been to Galway? It's right over on the west coast of Eire, a harbour town giving on to the Atlantic. You can't set foot in the town without wondering about what lies beyond the sea. Next stop: New York."

When we looked to Judith for confirmation, she nodded.

"Plenty of Irish Catholics, too, and Mary was a Catholic. That explains her reluctance to reveal her child's illegitimacy, as Earl has described to us, right down the generations to his. And if Lord Bunting had given her enough to live on, why haul herself through the humiliating experience of airing her guilty secrets? The church might even have tried to separate her from her baby. By posing as a widow, she was already happier and more secure than she had ever dreamed of being when she was growing up in an impoverished Irish community."

"Enough is as good as a feast," said Oriana abruptly, which surprised me coming from her.

Judith stood up and began to pace up and down.

"So, class, what can we conclude from the historical evidence? A – that the journal is genuine. B – that the records in the butler's flat corroborate Mary's presence at St Bride's. C – that Earl, with red hair beneath his brown dye –" Oriana shot me a reproachful look for having blabbed that confidence to Judith, which was unfair considering that her observation had only confirmed what I'd already suspected "– is a plausible descendant of Lord Bunting's secret lover. And D – that Lord Bunting's cleverly worded will allows Earl the rights to the estate, which Mary's young son, Edmund O'Flaherty, might have claimed over a hundred years ago. By rights, St Bride's School for Girls should never have come into being. And finally, point E – well, you can work out point E for yourselves: we're all stuffed."

I was not the only one in the room to find my eyes filling with tears. To my embarrassment, my nose began to run copiously, and I fumbled in my jacket pocket for a

258

tissue, only to find a crumpled piece of paper. Oh well, I thought, better use that than let my nose drip.

As quietly as possible, I unfolded it ready for a discreet blow, but gasped when I saw what was written on it. I sniffed hard to preclude the need for a tissue, then looked up.

"Or maybe not," I announced, brightening. "Because judging by what's printed on this receipt, Earl Bunting bought this journal in October from a collector of old diaries on eBay."

Oriana leapt to her feet, her chair clattering to the floor behind her.

"The odious little toad! How dare he try to fool us all with his trumped-up claims to the nobility?"

Mavis harrumphed.

"If you'd asked me, I could have told you he was a charlatan. That dodgy accent, for a start, like an Englishman who's never been to the States trying to pass for a Hollywood film star. But what does it matter what I think? Oh no, not a jot. I'm only a humble geography teacher."

The Bursar steepled his fingers.

"Actually, what matters most is what the governors think. Even before they read the journal, they thought the will alone was sufficient evidence, backed up by the various certificates proving Earl's lineage. Plus of course he showed them his American passport to prove his own identity."

Mavis was still fuming.

"What do the governors know about passports? I bet it's a forgery."

I passed the receipt to the Bursar to read. He remained unconvinced.

"I'm sorry, everyone," he said, panning the room. "I'm afraid this receipt is a forgery. I can't believe this particular journal would turn up for sale on eBay just as Earl Bunting pitched up at St Bride's. We're going to need firmer evidence than that to make Miss Harnett and the governors reverse their decision."

Mavis let out a long groan.

"OK, I confess. I made it up this morning, based on a receipt I'd just had from an eBay buyer. But I thought it was worth a try. Anything to get rid of the wretched fellow."

I turned to her, aghast.

"Mavis! I can't believe you set me up like that, planting your fake receipt on me!"

But I couldn't help laughing, all the same.

"So it looks as if we're stuck with the dreadful man," concluded Judith.

"Yes, bleeding our coffers dry," muttered Mavis, and got up to head for the door, where the girls were lining up ready for the first lesson of the afternoon.

39

A Chance Meeting

"Max! Am I glad to see you!"

The following Monday, when I returned to the staffroom after lunch, Max was waiting for me, looking pleased with himself.

"Can we go somewhere to talk in confidence, Gemma? In principle, I don't mind the rest of the staff knowing what I've learned about Earl this weekend, but I don't want to risk any wind of it getting back to him before we've got to the critical stage."

I glanced longingly at Old Faithful, but Max's unusually animated expression suggested whatever he had to share with me would be far more stimulating than coffee.

"Where to, Max?"

He nodded towards the window.

"Weather's a bit rough for the gardens. Not that I mind, but you're not dressed for outdoors. Let's head up into the gods for privacy."

I had no idea where he meant, but I followed him up the marble stairs. At the far end of the corridor that served my House dormitories stood a low, narrow door in the wall, which I'd always presumed to be a disused cupboard. Whenever I'd tried the handle, it had been locked, so I'd thought no more about it as it was off-limits to the girls.

Now Max produced a large, ancient key and unlocked the little door amidst much creaking.

"Squeaking's not good for subterfuge. Next time I'll bring my oilcan."

He went first as he knew where the light switch was. A dim old-fashioned bulb provided just enough illumination for us to pick our way down a dusty passage to a second similar door.

"Why didn't I know about this space?" I queried. "In my capacity as Fire Officer, I mean."

All school staff had an 'Extra' allocated on arrival, and Fire Officer was mine. When Max didn't answer, I wondered where else was still a secret from me.

Beyond the second door lay a room so brightly lit by huge skylights that at first I could barely see. Blinking, I eventually made out a row of dusty trunks, a disintegrating wicker laundry basket overflowing with moth-eaten curtains, a battered dressmaker's dummy, chairs with a leg or a rung missing – in short, the random assortment of bric-a-brac one might expect to find stored in the attic of an old stately home after anything truly valuable had been sold.

Max produced from one of his pockets a white handkerchief so large that I wondered whether it had seen former service as a surrender flag. He laid it over one of the trunks and gestured to me to sit down before perching on a rickety worn-out piano stool opposite.

It had taken us so long to reach our hideaway that by then I was bursting to hear his news. I was also conscious that I was due back in my classroom in twenty minutes.

"So, spill the beans, Max."

Max allowed himself a rare smile.

"Anthony Fullerton is a fine fellow. He managed to get me in to visit Dent over the weekend. Seems Earl Bunting fits the description of a mysterious business partner that took Dent for a complete ride before absconding without a trace. Well, he's not an exact fit. The man Dent knew went by the name of Edmund O'Flaherty and had long orange curly hair and a dark unkempt beard. But Dent confirmed the features and build match exactly.

"Dent told me he had first struck up a relationship with O'Flaherty outside a church. Dent was driving one of his fleet himself that day as a regular driver was unwell. While he was waiting for the wedding to finish, Dent nipped behind a tree in the churchyard to answer a call of nature. When he returned to the white Rolls-Royce he was driving, he found O'Flaherty sitting in the driver's seat. Realising he'd left his keys in the ignition, assuming no-one would steal a wedding car from outside a church, Dent's first thought was that he'd caught an audacious thief red-handed, just as he was about to drive off."

I couldn't stop myself from interrupting.

"I bet he would have made off with it, too, if Dent had been absent any longer. Honestly, what sort of heel steals a wedding car from a wedding? The poor bride and groom! What a start to their married life to come out and find your getaway car's disappeared."

Max grinned.

"I don't think Dent's website listed it as a getaway car, but that term is more appropriate than you realise, as you'll soon see. Anyway, in a distinctive Irish accent, our friend gave Dent a cock-and-bull story that he'd seen some reprobate skulking around and had leapt into the driver's seat only to deter the would-be thief."

"My goodness, what a nerve!"

"Quite. Having thus established Dent's gullibility, Earl listened sympathetically to Dent's outpouring of his business woes. Getting his car stolen would have been the final straw for the struggling West Bradford Wedding Cars. Drowning in debt, Dent bemoaned the fact that he was reduced to driving cars himself when he should have been in the back office managing client bookings, hiring drivers, advertising for new business and keeping up with his paperwork."

"Don't tell me – Earl Bunting to the rescue!"

Max nodded.

"Poor Dent was a sitting duck for a scammer. Long story short, he allowed our Earl, posing as Edmund O'Flaherty, to take over the running of the business, managing salaries, road tax, insurance payments, garage bills, VAT and so forth, leaving Dent to do what he was good at: attracting bookings and running the staff rota.

"O'Flaherty suggested that in lieu of part of his salary, he would move into the small empty flat over the garage. Dent was only too pleased to accept, thinking of the money it would save him, rather than querying why his new friend was homeless. Dent's only reservation was O'Flaherty's appearance."

"Oh dear," I put in. "Mr Dent must have been very gullible – or very desperate."

Max shrugged.

"Although as we know to our cost, Earl or Edmund, or whatever his real name is, is a very good actor. With the long auburn curls and shaggy beard he had at the time, he came across as a bit of a hippy, a poor fit for the company's image. Rather than visit the barber's, O'Flaherty volunteered to remain in the back office, never meeting any clients, nor even the drivers."

I folded my arms and crossed my legs.

"I've always suspected Earl is smarter than he lets on."

"Exactly right, Gemma. Thus he was able to evade ever being seen by anyone involved in the business besides Dent. All the better to ensure none of Dent's drivers or clients would be able to identify him when his crimes came to light."

Max, who never sat still for long, got up to stretch, and began to pace up and down as he continued.

"As they inevitably did, Gemma. But only after O'Flaherty had pocketed vast sums of money that he had supposedly spent on all the associated costs of running a car hire firm. He also kept back the final week's wages that should have been paid to the drivers.

"The first Dent knew of his fraudulent behaviour was when O'Flaherty called in sick one Monday morning. Only then, searching for something in O'Flaherty's desk, did Dent discover a mountain of financial demand letters that had arrived in the post. It emerged that for months, ever since O'Flaherty's arrival, not a single bill had actually been paid. All the paperwork O'Flaherty had given him was fake, even down to the statements from the new bank account that he had opened on Dent's behalf, on the pretext of lower service charges. Fullerton told me the fake papers were indistinguishable from the real thing. No idea where O'Flaherty got them from, but Fullerton suspects he's working in league with an expert forger somewhere."

"Presumably that's how he acquired his American passport. I don't think he's American at all. That pose is just to put us off the trail of his previous misdemeanours and explain why he took so long to come forward to claim his inheritance. I take it that Earl, as O'Flaherty, wasn't really sick that day."

"Nope. Dent reckons he'd done a runner the day before, on the Sunday. The last time he saw him was on the Saturday evening after the last booking of the day had returned to his yard."

40

The Getaway Car

"Earl turned up here on a Monday," I remembered.

"The next wedding booking wasn't until the following Friday, so it was a few days before Dent noticed one of his cars was missing – a white Rolls-Royce."

"That's a bit lax," I said. "I suppose he must have had his hands full sorting through that dodgy paperwork."

"Worse was yet to come, Gemma. A few days later, Dent was arrested on charges of running a car hire firm without insurance, road tax, MOTs and goodness knows what else, putting his clients at considerable risk. I'm guessing O'Flaherty's parting shot was to shop Dent to the authorities to get them off his own scent."

"So, the white Rolls-Royce was a getaway car after all?"

"Got it in one, Gemma. Not that the police believed Dent, as no other soul involved in the running of the business had ever set eyes on O'Flaherty. Despite Fullerton's best efforts to gather evidence, the police found Edmund O'Flaherty about as credible as an imaginary friend. They thought Dent was making the whole thing up to mask his own incompetence.

"Poor Dent didn't stand a chance. He was the company director, and his wife was company secretary, but hers was a token appointment. She played no part in the running of the business. Fullerton managed to get her let off with a caution, although she's likely to be banned from serving as a company director for ten years. Dent received less leniency. He's now on remand awaiting sentencing."

For a man normally of few words, Max had told a detailed and compelling story.

"Oh my word, Max, this is too good to be true! Well, for us, anyway, not for the unfortunate Mr Dent. Max, are you sure this isn't just a weird coincidence?"

A self-satisfied grin spread over Max's face.

"Far too much evidence to the contrary. Firstly, Dent gave an unequivocal confirmation that the images from my security cameras, taken from all angles, were of O'Flaherty. Earl's distinctive profile can't be masked by a change of hairstyle.

"Dent also identified Earl's vehicle from my description. When you were checking it after the girls' attack, I noticed a few minor blemishes. He described them all perfectly. Apart from those tiny distinguishing scrapes and scratches, he referred to a freak ridge in the rear left bumper that could only be the result of a one-off manufacturing flaw. I've checked Earl's car since I returned and found the exact same flaw."

"What about the BLISS licence plate?"

"Fake, as we'd suspected, knocked up out of hours on the branded platemaking machine in Dent's office. Apparently Dent had a marketing gimmick of presenting each bridal couple who used his services with a souvenir licence plate bearing their surname, for decorative purposes only, obviously. Edmund O'Flaherty had been trained how to use it. Making the souvenir plates was one of his many back-office chores."

He pulled a tin flask of water from a pocket and took a quick swig.

"You know what, Max? The scary thing is, Earl might have got away with it if he hadn't taken the lazy way out of hiding the car's origins. If he'd just made new plates without the company name, we'd never have spotted the Bradford connection."

"Luckily Dent's machine had only one template, which included the company name, so he'd have had to go elsewhere for a plain one. Blame a fatal combination of laziness and arrogance. He's not the first crook to kid himself he's smarter than everyone else, nor will he be the last. Fullerton said that if Al Capone had bothered to file accurate tax returns, he might never have gone to jail."

"So, what happens next, Max? Apart from afternoon lessons."

"First of all, please keep all this to yourself. We don't want Earl doing another moonlight flit if he thinks we're on to him."

"I'd think it unlikely, given that he now thinks he owns the place."

"Secondly, now that we've got the facts, I've got no qualms about putting it all in the hands of the law.

Fullerton is filing a report with the authorities on our behalf as we speak."

There was one thing that still puzzled me.

"I don't get why Earl even bothered with small-time fraud like that when he knew he had a legal claim to St Bride's. Why chase after small rewards elsewhere when he had the jackpot waiting for him here?"

"I'm guessing he didn't know about St Bride's until recently, when your predecessor made her ill-judged shout-out on social media. He's told us himself it was only by chance he found out about the image she'd shared of Lord Bunting's portrait when a friend spotted it and noticed the similarity to Earl. I wouldn't be surprised if that friend turns out to be his forger chum, spotting potential gain for himself. Not knowing the genuine connection, he probably saw it as another juicy opportunity for fraud and blackmail."

"Blackmail? How would that come into it?"

"If the forger provided fake documents to help Earl stake his claim, he'd then have a hold over him. He'd be seeking a regular sweetener from Earl in return. Earl would have no choice but to pay up if he wanted to keep the estate."

"Do you think the forger also faked Mary O'Flaherty's journal? Surely not, when Earl was already calling himself O'Flaherty. That would be too much of a coincidence."

Max shook his head.

"No, the journal's genuine enough, as are the will and the certificates of birth, death and marriage that connect Earl to Lord Bunting via Mary. The journal had probably been sitting unopened in someone's attic for generations, especially as Mary O'Flaherty considered it proof of a shameful secret, as did her descendants. Only Earl was ready to betray his ancestor's wishes for his own gain."

"In that case, I wonder why she didn't just destroy it?"

Max shrugged.

"Sentiment? Insurance? Pride? It's anyone's guess."

"Maybe Mary O'Flaherty really loved Lord Bunting and didn't want to sully the precious memory of their relationship."

Max grimaced. "That's more your area than mine, Gemma."

"Don't let Rosemary hear you say that," I teased.

"Anyway, it'll soon be game over for Earl Bunting. We just have to keep quiet about it and wait for the police to pick their moment to step in."

That was a disappointment. I couldn't wait to break the good news to my colleagues that their jobs and their accommodation were safe, at least for now.

"Can't we even tell Miss Harnett in confidence to put her out of her misery? Especially as it's Christmas. We're nearly at the end of term, and it would be so much nicer for her to be able to spend the holidays worry free, rather than wondering whether she'll even have a school to come back to in the new year."

"No can do, Gemma. I'm only telling you because you put me on to the car business in the first place. And don't get too excited, this is still potentially only a short-term solution. Fullerton reckons Earl's claim to the estate may be valid, although he's going to do his best to find a means to overturn it. He told me last night he thinks he's made a breakthrough that might solve all our problems, but he couldn't say more than that."

I wondered how much a lawyer like Fullerton might charge for his time.

"Have you checked with the Bursar that there's a budget to cover Fullerton's fees?" I asked warily.

Max waved a hand dismissively.

"Oh, no worries there, Gemma. Fullerton is so pleased that we've produced the evidence he needs to free his client, and to restore his own professional pride and reputation, that he won't charge us a penny."

Even tucked away in this attic room, we could hear the school bell summoning the girls to class. Max glanced at his watch then beckoned me follow him back the way we'd come in.

"Just think of Fullerton as this year's Secret Santa," he said as he locked the door behind us. "I promise you the outcome will be worth the wait."

41

Tidings of Comfort and Joy

It was all I could do to keep Max's new intelligence to myself for the next few days, especially when Joe kept asking me why I was looking so happy. I'm dreadful at dissembling.

"Oh, you know, just enjoying all the school's festivities," I said on the Thursday, the day before the end of term. "I haven't felt this Christmassy in years. Not surprising really, when the girls seem to have been preparing for it since half term, what with all the choir practice and nativity rehearsals and cookery and decorations."

By then we had festooned the classrooms and dormitories with home-made paperchains and an apparently inexhaustible supply of fairy lights. A huge fragrant fir tree, glistening with antique silver baubles, dominated the assembly hall, even eclipsing Lord Bunting's portrait. You couldn't go anywhere in the school without hearing a snatch of a Christmas carol being sung by one or more girls. Their tunes were usually more accurate than their words, but more than once, the distant sound of clear, pure voices harmonising had moved me to tears.

"You might like to come carol-singing with the sixth formers tonight in Wendlebury Barrow," said Joe, after I'd found myself joining in with a rendition of 'O Come All Ye Faithful' as we were leaving the Trough after lunch. "I'm going."

"Really? I didn't think carol-singing was your kind of thing?"

"And why shouldn't it be? Actually, you're quite right, it isn't, but I just want to do my bit for the girls. PE doesn't really lend itself to festive lessons and I don't get involved in the Christmas Fair other than to set up and take down the tables for the stalls, so as to steer clear of the girls' parents." He still kept a low profile when any members of the public were about. "I did try to get a Santas v Elves hockey match going, with the teachers as Santas and the girls as Santa's little helpers, but hey, you can't get the staff."

He didn't laugh at his own joke. He must have been worrying about losing his safe haven at St Bride's and returning to public life, where hostile press might still set traps for him. I tried to cheer him up.

"So which part do you sing, Miss Spryke, soprano or alto?"

"Neither. I'm just designated driver for the minibus. The Head of Music hasn't got a van licence."

"So you can drive, then?"

I'd only ever seen him ride his bike.

"Of course, if needs must, although if you ask me, it's two wheels good, four wheels bad." He waited for his *Animal Farm* reference to sink in. "But I don't think I could fit a dozen sixth formers on my cross-bar."

"Oh, I don't know. Two on the cross-bar, one in the saddlebag, one in each pannier and the rest forming a human pyramid on your shoulders?"

At last he cracked a smile.

"OK, clever clogs, but tonight it's the minibus or nothing. And we've a space if you'd like to come."

The thought of an evening in Wendlebury Barrow with Joe was appealing, even in the company of a dozen young chaperones.

"What does it involve exactly?"

"Nothing too onerous. The village is very pretty at this time of year, lit up with fairy lights and holly wreaths on every cottage door. We just traipse round the village streets, pausing at strategic points as dictated by tradition – on the village green by the big Christmas tree; outside the houses of a couple of former St Bride's pupils; at the homes of elderly residents too frail to attend the church carol service."

"I see, a captive audience!"

He smiled again.

"You've got it. Ending with a final gig in the pub to warm us up, rewarded with a free drink – a large glass of wine for the staff, a small one the girls who have already turned 18, and soft drinks for the under 18s and the driver."

I pictured the scene: The Bluebird's glowing fire, the bar decked out with holly and ivy and crowded with villagers full of the Christmas spirit, with the added benefit for me of being escorted by Joe. I wouldn't miss it for the world.

"Thanks, Joe, I'd love to."

"Great." He zipped up his mauve fleece ready for the chilly walk back to his pavilion. "Meet you in the entrance hall at 7.30pm." Then, as he went out the door, he turned to call over his shoulder, grinning: "I'll save you a place on the roof rack."

* * *

Although hearing the younger girls sing around school was charming, the more mature voices of the sixth formers carried much better outdoors. The air was crisp and cold, but by the time we reached our final stop at the village green, we were positively glowing from a combination of exercising our lungs for the past hour and being on the receiving end of appreciative remarks from everyone we'd sung to.

Several of the elderly men and women whose houses we'd stopped at had come out on to their doorsteps to hear us better, rapt smiles on their faces, applauding at the end and asking for more. Others had pulled back their curtains or opened their shutters, waving their thanks and blowing kisses through the window.

Such an enthusiastic audience built my confidence. I'd always sung in choirs at school, but had barely sung a note for years, and only ever in my head when my ex-boyfriend

Steven was around, as he would complain about my voice. During the course of the evening, my contribution had morphed from shy soprano, barely mouthing the words as I stared self-consciously at the carol sheets, to belting out the descant to 'O Come, All Ye Faithful', our last piece before entering the pub. As my voice soared, I lifted my face to the cloudless sky, which seemed to have cleared especially for us, admiring the abundant stars.

"Blimey, that was a revelation," whispered Joe over my shoulder. If I had realised he was standing right behind me, I might not have let my voice run away with me so much, but I was glad I had. It was good to feel I could be myself with Joe.

A short girl in a silver tinsel halo raised her hand.

"So, can we go to the pub now, miss? Please, miss?"

Louisa Humber the music teacher, checked her watch.

"OK, girls, you've done St Bride's proud. But no drinks till we've given The Bluebird three good carols!"

The girls all sighed as if that would be a dreadful chore, but I for one was glad our recital wasn't over.

As Louisa led the way into The Bluebird, a resounding cheer of recognition rose up from its customers. From behind the bar, Donald gave our group a friendly wave.

"Come on, girls, let's be having you. Can you start with my favourite, please?"

Louisa didn't need to ask what it was. I wondered for how many years she'd been bringing the school choir to The Bluebird. 'Three Kings from Persian Lands Afar' was soon reverberating around the bar, allowing the altos to eclipse the sopranos. Not a word was spoken until we'd finished, not even by Billy, the garrulous old boy I'd met in the bookshop earlier in the term, now ensconced in the corner with his cronies over a game of dominoes.

The contemplative calm continued with our rendition of 'Silent Night', first verse in the original German, before we upped the pace for 'The Holly and the Ivy'. After that, Donald beckoned us to the bar, where a dozen small glasses of white wine and several big ones were lined up for us, dwarfed by Joe's pint of bitter lemon.

Only then did our tight circle disperse. I was pleased to spot a few familiar faces. Hector and Sophie from the bookshop were in a booth, enjoying plates of glistening fish and chips, and they waved at me in greeting. With them was an older woman who I thought I'd seen visit the school now and again. I guessed she was the one who had recently brought a pair of peacocks to live in the school grounds.

Joe took my arm and steered me over to chat to them. The older woman held out her hands in welcome.

"Hello, my dears, that was delightful. I'm Kate, by the way, Hector's godmother. I gather you're Gemma, the new Head of English. I'm looking forward to your Christmas Fair tomorrow."

Sophie wrinkled her nose.

"Sorry I can't come to support it too, but we're expecting a busy day in the shop."

"I'll bring you and Hector back some of the girls' delicious mince pies," said Kate.

But before she could say any more, the front door flew open and a familiar figure strode in, heading straight for the bar, elbowing his way past the little gaggles of girls who were talking amongst themselves over their precious glasses of wine.

Hector caught my eye.

"There he is. That's him. The chap I told you about who was asking for the book about wills."

Joe and I exchanged glances.

"Oh my, is there no escape from you pesky kids?" Earl was saying as he leaned on the bar.

"Is he secretly a Scooby-Doo villain?" Hector whispered to me, making me nearly choke on my wine.

"I'm sure he didn't have that American accent when he came into our shop," added Sophie. "What's he playing at?"

One of the bolder girls going from table to table with our charity collection box strode up to Earl.

"Would you like to make a donation for the homeless, Mr Bunting?"

The room fell silent as she fixed him with her most winning smile. Encouraged by the girl's confidence, Donald leaned over the bar towards Earl.

"And while you've got your hand in your pocket, perhaps you'd like to settle your longstanding bar tab, Mr Bunting?"

Earl started, looking from Donald to the sixth former, as if suspecting them of being in league together. Then he grabbed the charity box from the girl's hand, to gasps of horror from all around.

"You want my tab settled? Well, back in the States we have a very useful saying: charity begins at home. I think the contents of this box should cover it. If not, you have only the mean spirits of your customers to blame."

"I think you'll find that's called theft," piped up the girl he'd snatched it from.

Donald fished in his pocket for a five-pound note and stuffed it into the charity box before returning it to her.

I was thankful Oriana wasn't on Earl's arm this evening.

In the silence that followed, Earl stared at Billy's posse, who had been quaffing his champagne this last couple of months. Billy pulled a pack of cards from the pocket of his grubby tweed jacket and began to shuffle them.

"OK, boys, who's for a game of gin rummy?"

When they turned their backs on Earl, his face flushed dark red and he strode stiffly to the door, slamming it behind him.

"Oh well, at least he won't have to add drink driving to his charge sheet," I said as soon as he was out of earshot.

"Charge sheet? What charge sheet?" asked Hector. "What's he done?"

Remembering myself, I waved my hand dismissively.

"Sorry, just my silly joke."

Louisa Humber returned to the centre of the bar and clapped her hands.

"Now, how about a bit of community singing?" she said, her clear teacher's voice commanding even Billy's attention. "Anyone for 'We Three Kings'? Official lyrics only, please!"

42

All's Fair

"Tragic to think this might be St Bride's last ever Christmas Fair," grumbled Mavis as she set out her department's stall in the assembly hall. Mavis's pupils had been covering plain glass Christmas tree baubles with cuttings from old maps.

"I've been thinking that all month, every time one of the school's festive traditions takes place," replied Joe, who was setting up a trestle table for my stall next to Mavis's.

"The last Christmas tree arriving, the last decorations going up, the carol singing to the villagers last night," she added.

"But Mavis, you never go out with the carol singers," said Joe.

Mavis slammed a wooden crate of her stock so hard on her table that it was a wonder the glass didn't shatter. The girls must have used strong glue.

"No, but I could have done if I'd wanted. And the important thing is, the villagers enjoyed it. It'll be their loss too."

I tried to placate them both.

"No school is an island," I said brightly, admiring a bauble covered in Madagascar. It would have been a shame to spoil the school's last Christmas Fair by squabbling. Although from my recent conversation with Max, I was hopeful there'd be many more to come.

Once Joe had clicked the tabletop into place on its legs and a Year 7 had tested its stability by jumping on it, I began to lay out my department's contribution to the event: handmade Christmas cards featuring quotes from Charles Dickens. Colouring printouts of John Leech's original illustrations of *A Christmas Carol* had kept my younger classes quiet while we'd enjoyed the audiobook of this timeless classic, a very soothing end to the busy term. Inside each card they'd written their favourite quotes from the story. I'd hoped more would choose "God bless us, every one!" than "Bah, humbug", but the latter might please anyone less than keen on the traditional festivities. Every family has its Scrooge.

Next Joe set to work on Felicity's stall which was to be on the other side of mine. Organised as ever, Felicity had already stacked numerous tins and plastic boxes of baked goods on the floor. The minute her table was up, she threw over it a beautiful tablecloth, hand-embroidered with wreaths of holly and ivy. Her star pupil Issy dealt gold-edged white plates out in neat lines and topped them with paper doilies, which Felicity then piled high with pyramids of mince pies and gingerbread stars. Issy dusted the whole display with caster sugar from an antique silver shaker, sparkling grains falling down on every plate like high-speed snow.

Meanwhile, Joe was setting up a second table for Felicity, which she swiftly covered with another festive cloth, this one embroidered with golden stars. Moments later, a procession of sixth formers filed across the hall from the direction of the courtyard, each reverently holding in front of her, like the Three Kings bearing gifts, a round silver board displaying a handmade Christmas cake.

As they delivered their cakes to Felicity's second table, I admired their handiwork. Each girl had been given free rein to decorate her cake, and each cake was different. My favourite was the traditional nativity scene with stable walls assembled from slabs of chocolate, bumpy side outwards to represent bricks, and with a thatch of Shredded Wheat.

When the last cake had been set on the table, the young chefs stood by, confident of compliments. I found something nice to say about each one, although some needed explanation.

"What's a beach scene got to do with Christmas?"

I pointed to a cake topped with white-crested azure waves populated by Playmobil surfers.

"It's what we do at Christmas where I come from, miss," said the tall blonde girl holding it. She pointed to a pile of oyster shells, saved from a previous cookery lesson, scrubbed clean and arranged at one side of the cake. "See? That's Sydney Opera House."

"And this one? It's very pretty. I like the subtle use of colour. Those sparkles of green, pink and yellow against the navy-blue royal icing are spectacular, but where's the Christmas connection?"

An even blonder girl pointed to a tiny red speck that I hadn't noticed amongst the swirls of colour.

"See? That's Santa, passing through the Northern Lights on Christmas Eve."

Felicity smiled proudly. Somehow, she'd brought out the girls' individual characters while they adhered to the rigid instructions required for successful baking.

Issy set down a price card on the cake stall, the letters and numbers made of icing piped on to a slab of gingerbread.

"I can't believe you can bear to part with your beautiful cakes after all the work that's gone into them," I said. "I certainly couldn't if I'd made something so wonderful."

"Don't worry, miss. There's an unwritten rule that our parents have first refusal on the cake made by their daughter." Issy pointed to the identifying initials on each silver base. "Besides, it's for a good cause."

I smiled.

"Of course it is. To help pay for Christmas dinners at the homeless shelter in Slate Green, same as the carol singing last night."

Earl strolled up to join us.

"You mean today's takings aren't in aid of school funds either?" He scowled. Perhaps he'd been hoping to claim his tithe.

To my horror, he then came round behind my table, dragged one of the chairs allocated to me to the gap between Felicity's stall and mine, and planted himself down.

Felicity smiled sweetly at him.

"Oh, how kind of you, Earl. You've come to help us!"

I had to turn away and fake a cough to hide my laughter. When I'd recovered, I addressed Issy, who was still tweaking the arrangements of the cakes.

"Could you do me a favour, please, Issy, and keep an eye on my stall for moment? I'd just like to have a look round before we let the public in."

There was no way I was going to trust Earl with my wares.

"Of course, miss."

She came to stand at the other end of my table, as far as she could get from Earl.

My tour of the other stalls was as much to avoid Earl as to go shopping. If he was planning to spend the whole Fair beside me, I needed to steel myself to bear his company for that long.

Only when I reached the far end of the hall and was turning away from the Music department stall, selling CDs of the girls singing carols, did I realise why Earl was so keen on that particular spot. He'd positioned his chair precisely beneath Lord Bunting's portrait. Visitors could not fail to remark on the resemblance and enquire as to their relationship. Doubtless he welcomed any attention that would compound his right to the estate.

I headed next for Judith Gosling's stall, displaying small framed pieces of parchment bearing festive slogans. She'd used her last week's lessons to pass on her calligraphy skills to her pupils. I picked up one saying

"Comfort and Joy", lettered in red, gold and green, with corner details in the form of generously-berried holly sprigs.

"I know the Fair's not officially open for business yet, but could I buy this one, please, Judith? It would make a lovely Christmas gift for my parents."

Judith whisked it off the table, swathed it in red tissue, and labelled it with my name.

"Can I tell Abigail I've sold her handiwork to you? She'll be thrilled."

"Of course. By the way –" I motioned in Earls' direction, without looking directly at him, in case he was watching me "– do you see what I see?"

Earl had now arranged his pose to exactly match Lord Bunting's in the painting.

She squinted across the hall.

"Oh, good grief! I hope no-one else notices."

I fished my purse out of my pocket and handed over a ten-pound note.

"Well, I for one don't plan to introduce him to anyone. Let's hope Felicity's beautiful cakes – and my department's cards – distract visitors from noticing him."

A rattle at my side heralded the arrival of the Bursar, carrying a fir-green enamel bucket filled with plastic bank bags of mixed coin. He dropped one on Judith's table.

"Here's your float, Miss Gosling. Miss Lamb, to your table, please. I can't give you your float unless you're at your stall."

Judith and I exchanged weary glances at his officiousness.

"I'll catch you later, Gemma. Have fun, and don't eat too many mince pies. It's a mixed blessing to have your stall next to Felicity's. If you're not careful, you'll have gained half a stone by the time the Fair closes."

I had to run back to my stall to beat the Bursar. I'd only just transferred my float into my takings tin when the school bell sounded, marking the Fair's official opening by our special guest, the vicar of Wendlebury Barrow.

Joe, his work done, stepped across to my stall.

"I'd better scarper now. You know Hairnet's policy about me not fraternising with parents at close quarters."

It seemed a shame for him to miss all the excitement of the Fair, but he must have felt it was a reasonable price to pay for safe haven from the prying eyes of the press. The local paper had sent a photographer who was already snapping away.

The double doors from the entrance hall were flung open and the two youngest girls in the school, Imogen and Abigail, stood either side, each holding the ends of a gold ribbon stretched across the threshold. The vicar proceeded to cut the ribbon with a large pair of Felicity's dressmaking shears.

Immediately, the hall began to fill with a mixture of local residents and girls hanging on to their parents' arms, pink-cheeked with excitement at being reunited and at the prospect of the long school holidays ahead. Within minutes, the hall was heaving, and all the stalls, including mine, were doing a roaring trade. Spotting more familiar faces from Wendlebury Barrow – the vicar's wife and Hector's godmother, Kate – filled me with a warm glow of belonging in the school's wider community.

* * *

Half an hour later, Judith, leaving her stall in the capable hands of a pair of sixth formers, snaked her way through the crowds towards Felicity.

"Quick, Felicity, what's the sweetest thing you've got?"

Her abrupt request interrupted a father's purchase of a box of mince pies. Appraising her with a glance, Felicity, whose Extra was as First Aider, realised Judith was asking for medical reasons. She passed her customer's banknote to Issy to finish the transaction.

"Are you hypo, Judith? I'm sorry, I've no fast-acting carbs on my stall. But here, take my seat, and I'll nip to the tearoom and get you a juice."

The Trough had been turned into a festive tearoom for a day, complete with Santa's grotto in one corner to delight younger siblings. Santa was, of course, the Bursar. We weren't exactly spoilt for choice for candidates to play old men. Max could have concealed plenty of presents in his trousers, but he had other duties to worry about with so many visitors on site. I hoped that the Bursar was enjoying himself. His young visitors' adoration and their appreciation of his generosity would make a nice change for him.

Judith slumped gratefully on to Felicity's chair, pale as the pastry on the mince pies, her forehead damp with sweat. She glanced up at me apologetically and forced a smile.

"Sorry, Gemma, low blood sugar. Need carbs. Occupational hazard of diabetes. I'll be fine once I've had a drink of juice."

This confused me.

"I thought you said mince pies were full of sugar. Won't one of those do?"

She helped herself to a paper serviette from the pile on the corner of Felicity's table and wiped her forehead.

"Yes, they are, and other carbs too, but the fat content slows the digestion. Takes too long for the sugar to hit the bloodstream. I usually carry glucose tablets in my pocket, but I changed jackets before the Fair and forgot to transfer them across."

"You refused mince pies in the staffroom the other day too, didn't you? I thought maybe you just didn't like them."

"I'm not that keen on them, to be honest. They're so carb heavy that they send my blood sugar sky high. They're not worth the bother."

Felicity returned with a glass of orange juice.

"Here you go, Judith. Stay there till you feel better. It looks as if your sixth formers are doing a good job on your stall."

Judith drained the glass in one long swig.

"Thanks, Felicity, you're a pal."

She sat back and closed her eyes, only to be disturbed by another emergency alert for Felicity.

"Miss Button, Miss Button!"

A Year 9 came running up to accost her.

"Please can you come to see my pa. He says his car's making a funny noise so I told him you could fix it."

Felicity sighed.

"Of course, Bryony. Gemma, please will you keep an eye on my stall in case Issy gets overloaded?"

"Sure."

Issy was boxing up each cake as it was sold, deftly assembling flat-packed cardboard boxes with machine-like efficiency. I wasn't sure my origami skills would be up to it.

Earl reminded me of his presence with a cough.

"Earl, wouldn't you like to visit the tearoom?"

He hadn't budged since the Fair opened.

"Don't worry, miss, I can order something to be brought to him, if he likes," said Issy.

"That's very kind of you, Issy," I replied, in the absence of any show of gratitude from Earl. "I don't suppose you could manage a cup of tea for me too, could you, please? That would be wonderful."

"I'll recruit some of the little ones. They love playing waitresses. These two will do."

She came out from behind her stall to capture Imogen and Abigail, who were loitering nearby, whispering and giggling to each other. Each was wearing a makeshift halo fashioned from the gold ribbon cut by the vicar. They were probably making the most of their last afternoon together for a month – the downside of the long Christmas break. Issy looped her arms around their narrow shoulders, and a moment later the two little girls were trotting purposefully across the hall to the Trough.

Judith, meanwhile, had resumed her normal colour, and now returned to her stall.

Earl shifted in his seat. He must have had cramp after holding the same position for so long. He was probably also bored. Hardly any visitors had stopped to talk to him, more interested in their daughters after weeks of separation.

"What was all that about?"

"What was all what about?"

He jabbed a finger in the direction of Judith's stall.

"That history teacher. Rejecting all that delicious baked stuff in favour of a glass of juice."

"It's because she's diabetic. You know, like Lord Bunting's son. It was a medical emergency. She needed to sit down and recover."

The mention of his supposed ancestor perked him up.

"Oh yes, of course. That allergy business. Runs in our family. I'm a martyr to it myself."

Why did he always have to turn everything back to himself? He was such a bad listener, too. A term as pupil at St Bride's would have improved his manners as well as restraining his ego.

Just in time to stop me delivering a sharp retort to Earl, the two Year 7s reappeared in front of us. Imogen bore a tray with two bone china teacups, saucers, teapot, milk jug and sugar bowl, which she set down carefully in a space on Felicity's table, already almost empty after a flurry of sales.

Abigail held out a plate of selected pastries, offering it first to me, although Earl was already reaching out for it. I chose a finger of Christmas cake. Then Earl took a mince pie with one hand, and with the other grabbed a gingerbread Santa sporting thick red and white icing.

When he stuffed the mince pie into his mouth in one go, the girls' jaws dropped in horror at his bad manners.

After chewing for a bit, he asked through a flurry of crumbs, "For gosh sakes, what is this? I thought it was an apple pie."

Imogen sounded proud.

"It's a mince pie, Mr Earl. It's one of our best things about Christmas in England."

He clutched at his throat.

"A mince pie? Like the one that the history teacher couldn't eat? My God! Help me! I've been poisoned!"

Spitting a shower of crumbs, he fell headlong on to the floor, coughing dramatically.

Imogen and Abigail turned to me, wide-eyed.

"Honestly, miss, it really is just a mince pie. We didn't poison it. We didn't even spit on it."

Abigail bent to pick up the gingerbread Santa that had fallen on the floor and lay it on Earl's saucer for later.

"Murder! Murder! Call the police!" Earl was shouting.

The room fell silent as everyone turned to stare at him. There were gasps of horror and sympathy. Felicity, returning from her mechanic's duties, dashed over to kneel beside him.

"What's happened, Earl? Are you choking? Sit up and I'll give you the Heimlich manoeuvre."

Her voice was calm and reassuring. She got behind him and hauled him into a sitting position, her arms around his chest, hands locked together beneath his solar plexus.

"Wait a minute, Felicity, I don't think that's the problem. Earl?"

His eyes bulging, he pointed to his mouth, still full of crumbs.

"Di - a – be - tic."

Felicity frowned and let go of him, and he dropped back on to the floor.

"What nonsense. If you're diabetic, one mince pie won't do you any harm. Not if you take your insulin. It might put your blood sugar up, but it won't kill you."

I looked round for Issy.

"Issy, can you find Bunty? Her dad's a doctor. Can you bring him over, just to be on the safe side, please? Tell him a diabetic's in trouble."

Abigail began to sob.

"I haven't murdered someone, have I?"

I went over to put my arms around the quaking child and whisper some words of comfort.

"No, don't worry, he's fine. He's just showing off, attention seeking. Honestly, I think he missed his vocation as an actor."

Now that he had the eyes of the whole crowd, people started to look from Earl to the portrait and back again, asking each other questions.

A man in a smart suit cut through the throng from the direction of the entrance, his daughter Bunty lugging her father's medical bag a step behind him. She set it down beside him and opened it with the assurance of a magician's lovely assistant. Plunging his hand into its depths, he pulled out a small zipped case from which he withdrew a tiny black electronic device, a single-use lancet and a white plastic test strip of the kind I'd seen Judith use in the staffroom before lunch. He slid the test strip into the device, one end of it protruding.

"Suspected hyperglycaemia, eh?" he said, taking Earl's forefinger and jabbing it to produce a bead of blood, wicking it up with the end of the test strip. "Been overdoing the sweeties, sir?"

Suddenly a distinctive sound drowned out the murmurs of consternation about us – the unmistakeable two-tone whine of a siren.

"My goodness, that was fast," the doctor was saying as he took Earl's pulse. "I haven't even called 999. Are the local emergency services psychic in these parts, Bunty? I'm afraid the paramedics will have had a wasted journey. There's nothing wrong with this gentleman that I can see."

Bunty beamed with pride at her father's nonchalance in the face of a crisis. After checking the reading, he dropped the test kit back into his case.

"Your blood glucose is in normal range, sir. Are you sure you're diabetic? Any other symptoms at all? All your vital signs seem fine."

He seized Earl's arm to help him stand up, then guided him back to his chair, looking at him quizzically. Earl pointed to the portrait above him.

"A family trait, we're a martyr to it," he began.

Before he could explain any further, a pair of uniformed policemen marched into the hall, boots clomping across the parquet floor. They were escorted by Max, who was pointing in Earl's direction.

The shorter of the policemen marched up to Earl with a diagnosis of his own.

"Earl Bunting, also known as Edmund O'Flaherty, I am arresting you on suspicion of fraudulent behaviour with regard to West Bradford Wedding Car Company. You do not have to say anything, but…"

"OK, girls, nothing to see here," Felicity proclaimed, positioning herself between Earl and the throng that had gathered around him. "Getting arrested is one life skill I hope none of you will ever need."

Miss Harnett appeared from nowhere to stand beside me – it was as if she'd been taking lessons from McPhee – and clapped her hands for silence, as she did before our daily assembly.

"Ladies and gentlemen, if you'd all be so kind as to proceed to the library, we'll close the term with our traditional carol service. Please collect a hymn sheet on your way in."

Earl bobbed about, trying to struggle free of the policeman's sturdy grip.

"You're not getting rid of me this easily, you stupid old bat. You know my claim to the estate is real. You'll see!"

His American accent had vanished, his speech now as English as mine.

Max addressed Miss Harnett.

"I wouldn't take any notice of this scallywag if I were you, Headmistress. He's just living proof that decency and good manners are not genetically determined."

Miss Harnett turned to the police officers.

"Thank you so much, officers. Now, if you'll bear with me a moment, I'll have some of our girls' home-made mince pies boxed up for you to take back to the station.

I'm sure you and your colleagues will find them absolutely delicious."

With a gracious smile and a regal wave at the writhing Earl, she headed for the library.

43

The Christmas Present

"So, tell me, Max, is Earl really a descendant of Lord Bunting?" In gratitude at his role in detaining Earl, Miss Harnett had invited Max to sit beside her at the table.

The girls, their parents and the local residents had all gone home by now, and the staff had gathered in the teachers' dining room for our traditional end-of-term Christmas dinner. Max's wife Rosemary and her team had just served us a magnificent four-course festive meal, and we were relaxing over coffee and mints against the backdrop of a glowing log fire in the huge marble fireplace.

"Oh yes, Headmistress, he is related all right. Even though he had forged his American passport, the rest of the documentation was genuine, as was Mary O'Flaherty's son's claim to the estate."

"Mary O'Flaherty must have been a clever woman to negotiate such a great legacy," said Miss Harnett.

297

"But not so clever as to have worked out that her son might not be the only one who stood to benefit from Lord Bunting's will," I put in. "You see, Max and I have discovered there was another heir produced in similar circumstances."

"Don't tell me Earl Bunting has a brother?" The Bursar put his face in his hands, forgetting the pink rash he'd incurred from Santa's beard.

"No, but Mary O'Flaherty's son did," said Max. "Or rather, a half-brother. The boys shared only a father. It seems Mary O'Flaherty was only one of a string of extra-marital liaisons, all carried out in the privacy of Honeysuckle Lodge."

The Bursar shifted uncomfortably in his chair and Miss Harnett became strangely engrossed with the contents of her empty coffee cup.

I chimed in to carry on with Max's revelation. "Before Mary O'Flaherty, Matilda Thompson, the previous occupant of Honeysuckle Lodge, also left the estate, never to return, for exactly the same reason."

Judith gasped. "Of course, it all makes sense! I was wondering why Lord Bunting's will pre-dated the first entry in Mary O'Flaherty's journal by two years. When he wrote it, he was making allowances for Matilda Thompson's unborn child. But when Lord Bunting showed Mary the will, she can't have noticed the date and just believed what she wanted to believe: that Bunting was providing for her child. But it wasn't that at all. Or it might even be the case that Mary O'Flaherty knew of Matilda's plight and realised that her own child would be only second in line to the estate. That's why she never bothered returning with him to try to stake a claim."

I looked at Max, and he gave me a slight nod to proceed.

"I'm pleased to say no matter how genuine Earl's descent, he has no claim to the estate. Because Matilda Thompson's line is still going, in the form of one Jeremy Shackleton, direct descendant of Lord Bunting's oldest surviving son, born out of wedlock to Matilda over a year before Mary O'Flaherty's baby."

Oriana, seated next to me, groaned and covered her face with her hands.

"Go on, Gemma, break it to me gently. What's this Jeremy Shackleton like? Where is he now, and does he know about this windfall he's about to have?"

She undid the clasp of the triple string of pearls around her neck and lay them on the table, as if drawing a line under her term as Jackie Kennedy.

I nodded to Max to prompt him for our final revelation. Max removed his napkin from his lap, placed it beside his coffee cup and rose to his feet.

"Funnily enough, he should be arriving here any minute now. Bear with me a moment."

Miss Harnett and the Bursar exchanged anxious glances as Max left the room. I leaned over to address them.

"Don't worry, it's all going to be fine." I felt I was about to burst with excitement. "You see, Jeremy Shackleton – or rather, Boon-Nam, as he prefers to be known these days – isn't a bit like Earl Bunting at all, even though Boon-Nam means 'one born with good fortune'."

"Oh no, not another weirdo with a multitude of disguises," grumbled Mavis. "Sorry, Oriana, I was referring to Earl or Edmund or whatever other names he's used in his dubious career. I didn't mean you."

Oriana's indignant response was curtailed by Max's return, accompanied by a beaming middle-aged man wearing small round wire glasses, a long robe the colour of satsumas, and rope sandals. His shaven head bore a brunette shadow. Over his arm he carried a neatly folded coarse crimson linen shawl. A battered chestnut leather satchel hung on a long strap across his body.

Miss Harnett leapt to her feet to greet him, pressing her palms together and offering a small bow, which he returned.

"Namaste, Bhante," she said, with a deferential smile. I wondered how often she'd had to greet a Buddhist monk before, as she seemed to know the etiquette.

"Please, Headmistress, just call me Boon-Nam," he said pleasantly. "Thank you for your kind welcome."

"The pleasure is ours, Boon-Nam. Now, you must be frozen. Would you care to come and sit by the fire?"

Having settled our visitor in one of the pair of fireside chairs, she sat down in the other, facing him. The Bursar came to stand behind her, resting his hands on the chair back. They reminded me of an old sepia photo of Victorian husband and wife. The rest of us got up to gather around them in a semi-circle.

In the flickering firelight, Max sought me out among the huddle of teachers. "Gemma, you're better with words than I am. Perhaps you'd like to explain."

I smiled, suddenly feeling a little shy.

"Yes, of course, Max. You see, when we provided Mr Dent's lawyer, Mr Fullerton, with the evidence to prove his client's innocence, he was so pleased that he offered to do whatever he could to help our cause. Max suggested that Mr Fullerton try to trace any descendants of Matilda Thompson's son. We thought there might be a more palatable alternative to Earl Bunting."

"He couldn't be much worse," grumbled Mavis.

"While obviously we'd rather the school remained the property of Miss Harnett, as it has been for so many years, we also wanted to know the truth, and thus guard against any more nasty surprises like the arrival of Earl Bunting."

Miss Harnett nodded.

"Yes, better to know the truth than fear what it might be."

"I hope I am not a nasty surprise," put in Boon-Nam, with a smile as sweet as any Year 7's. "Although the legacy was a surprise to me, too."

Before anyone might contradict him, I pressed on.

"You're certainly not, Boon-Nam, because, as Mr Fullerton has already explained to Max, your vow renouncing all material goods means you have no interest in taking over St Bride's. And now, thanks to the wonderful Mr Fullerton, you've specified in a legal statement that you are transferring all your rights in the estate back to Miss Harnett. Like your esteemed ancestor, you would prefer to see the estate run as a school, especially one like this that benefits so many young people, than for the sole enjoyment of a single owner."

Boon-Nam lifted the flap of his satchel and pulled out a large brown envelope bearing Miss Harnett's name and the school's address written in black fountain pen, the writing large, open-looped and clearly legible. Miss Harnett reached across the hearth to take it from him. Her voice quavered when she spoke.

"My dear man, this is the most wonderful Christmas present that anyone could hope for."

The monk beamed again.

"I am afraid that as a Buddhist, I do not celebrate Christmas, but I promise I will be happy on every day of the year for you, and for the many girls and staff in your care. This gesture makes me happier than owning the estate could ever do."

As Oriana passed her hand over her own thick bob, her eyes were fixed on Boon-Nam's shaven head.

"Orange isn't really my colour anyway," she said, more to herself than to him.

The Bursar was looking more cheerful than he had done since half term.

"So, what you're saying, Gemma, is that we've turned a pound's profit on the deal?"

With that, we all fell about laughing. Miss Harnett accepted the Bursar's handkerchief to mop her streaming eyes, and Mavis punched the air with surprising force.

But Judith had eyes only for Boon-Nam.

"I'm not sure how long you're planning to stay here, Boon-Nam, but would you mind awfully doing one more favour for us? It's tiny by comparison with what you've just done."

We all turned to stare.

"If you wouldn't mind accompanying me to the assembly hall, I'd love to take your photograph with the portrait of Lord Bunting, just for the archives."

Boon-Nam rose to his feet and shook the folds from his robes.

"Madam, I would be honoured. Though I do not suppose you will find I look much like him."

When he patted the dark shadow on his shaven head, we could hardly disagree. But the angle of his hand as it came to rest at his side and the twinkle in his kindly dark eyes were extraordinarily familiar.

* * *

As Judith, the Bursar and Miss Harnett escorted Boon-Nam to the assembly hall, the rest of us returned to the dining table to tackle the bottle of champagne that Max had somehow just conjured from a pocket in his ever-capacious trousers.

"I must say, my first Christmas at St Bride's has been full of surprises," I said, filling my glass and passing the bottle on. "What on earth might next term bring?"

A flurry of chatter broke out as each member of staff described their favourite aspect of the spring term. What I'd thought might prove the bleakest part of the school year started to sound like something to look forward to.

When Oriana got up to fetch a fresh pot of coffee from the kitchens, Joe slid into her chair beside me.

"So in the meantime, are you looking forward to seeing your parents at Christmas, Miss Lamb?"

At that moment, seeing Joe dressed in his civvies for a change — soft black jeans and a sky-blue sprigged pattern cotton shirt — what I was most looking forward to was catching him on his own so I could put my arms around him. But with the other staff still surrounding us, I held back.

"Yes, I am. And you?"

"Of course. I'll be staying with my parents for the whole of next week. And if you find yourself getting bored, remember my open invitation. My folks have plenty of spare rooms. You can come any time."

How I wanted to take him up on that offer, but then I thought of my parents and their welcoming hug, and of presenting them with my little gift of 'Comfort and Joy', and the souvenir mugs from Hector's House, and I was sure I was doing the right thing. Besides, I was looking forward to becoming better acquainted with Sparky, their new cat.

"Oriana told me she's going to ask the Bursar to stay with them for the whole of the holidays," he added.

I couldn't help but smile. I leaned very close to Joe to make sure only he could hear what I had to say next.

"So do you think the Bursar is really Oriana's father? And not that fabled governor at all?"

Joe's eyes twinkled mischievously.

"Don't you think you've done enough investigating for one term, Miss Lamb? If I told you, I'd have to kill you. And that would completely spoil my Christmas."

"But there's still New Year," I put in hopefully. "I haven't made any plans for New Year's Eve yet, have you?"

When Joe reached under the table and clasped my hand, I didn't resist.

"I have now. Merry Christmas, Gemma."

Acknowledgements

With grateful thanks to all those who helped, directly or indirectly, with the writing and production of this book:

Friends, former colleagues and past pupils of Westonbirt School, where I worked for thirteen years in rather different circumstances from Gemma Lamb's. The strength and warmth of its community spirit inspired me to invent St Bride's.

Belinda Holley for her advice about hockey sticks.

Joy Bell and her Leith's course students at Westonbirt School for their inspirational Christmas cake designs.

My hairdresser Natasha Harding of Head Start Studio for the insights into money for old rope on eBay.

My daughter Laura Young for telling me about the Medicis' secret passages in Florence.

My editor Alison Jack and cover designer Rachel Lawston, gifted, patient and generous professionals who I am very lucky to have as part of my team.

My pre-publication readers Lucienne Boyce and Belinda Holley and my proofreader Dan Gooding, whose vigilance saves me from myself.

Sir Frederick Banting, whose pioneering work with insulin continues to save the lives of countless people with Type 1 diabetes, including my husband and our only child.

My husband and daughter for their patience and moral support as I spend far too much family time at my desk.

Debbie Young

Stay in Touch

To receive news about new releases, special offers and a free ebook of *The Pride of Peacocks*, a short novella set in the world of Sophie Sayers and St Bride's, join my mailing list at www.authordebbieyoung.com. Your email address will never be used for any other purpose and you can unsubscribe at any time.

How to Make an Author's Day

If you have enjoyed *Stranger at St Bride's* or any other of my books, please consider leaving a brief review online. Book reviews help authors sell more books and reach more readers. Thank you very much for your support.

Also by Debbie Young

The Sophie Sayers Village Mysteries
Best Murder in Show
Trick or Murder?
Murder in the Manger
Murder by the Book
Springtime for Murder
Murder Your Darlings
Murder Lost and Found (coming soon)

Staffroom at St Bride's Stories
Secrets at St Bride's
Stranger at St Bride's
Scandal at St Bride's (coming soon)

Tales from Wendlebury Barrow
The Price of Peacocks (Readers' Club exclusive)
The Natter of Knitters
The Clutch of Eggs (coming soon)

Printed in Great Britain
by Amazon

81433136R00185